Kyna

A Story of Love

Lisa Washington

Library of Congress Control Number:

ISBN-13: 978-1-953205-02-5
ISBN-10: 1-953205-02-5

Washington Way Publishing
P.O. Box 1281
Pooler, GA
Printed in the United States of America
www.thewashingtonwayllc.com

DEDICATION

My Husband

I will be glad and rejoice in Your unfailing love, for You have seen my troubles, and You care about the anguish of my soul. (Psalm 31:7)

ACKNOWLEDGMENTS

Father God

Thank you to Ivy League Consulting

Gabrielle Topp

LaVeta Davenport

Chapter 1

Kyna Lové Hammond was small in size but mighty in passion. Her grandmother called her a warrior because of the fire in her spirit. She was younger than her sisters, but she protected them fiercely as if she were the oldest. So, when she stomped across the courtyard toward Dr. Grant Hawkins and his brother Morgan, she was a woman on a mission.

Morgan noticed movement from the corner of his eye. He turned to see who was heading in his direction and was immediately blown away by the beauty of the woman charging toward him. She was petite and flanked by two women who closely resembled her in height and facial features.

"What did you do to my sister?" Kyna accused Grant. Her other sisters Karleigh and Karmyn were not far behind her, wearing the same angry look as Kyna. Before Grant could respond to her question, she continued, "I told you to be careful with her. I told you to tell her the truth. Poe is not like the women you date. She is special."

Morgan was mesmerized by her passion and defense of her sister. Although her anger was currently directed at his brother, the fiery glint of her eyes were causing a stirring within him. His brother Grant and her sister Kaleigh, whom they affectionately called Poe, had been seeing each other up until now. An unfortunate event occurred that caused Kaleigh to leave the ceremony abruptly.

The group was currently standing just outside of the historic Warren Building that the Hawkins Group purchased to renovate as an upscale hotel. The ceremonial groundbreaking event had ended when a woman from Grant's past appeared and started to create drama.

"Don't you think I know how special she is? Kyna, I promise, I didn't want to hurt her. But I'll try my hardest to make this right. With her and with you," Grant promised.

"Well, you will have to get back in her good graces on your own. No help from me at all," Kyna pointed her finger into Grant's chest on the last word.

"Grant won't need any help. I think he knows what to do," Morgan said, making his presence known to the women who hadn't noticed him standing there.

Kyna rolled her eyes at Morgan, then scanned him from head to toe. Even her brazen discontentment toward Morgan was appealing to him.

"Ladies, this is my brother Morgan," Grant introduced him. Then, with a swing of his hand, he said to Morgan, "These are Kaleigh's sisters, Kyna, Karmyn, and Karleigh."

Kyna focused her eyes back on Grant. "You've got some work to do, Buddy. Good luck." She stormed off with her sisters right behind her.

"Whoa! She's a spitfire. You have to work with her every day?" Morgan rubbed his hand over his bald head.

"She is the smartest and most competent nurse I have ever worked with, and she pulls no punches. She does make work more interesting."

Morgan agreed with his brother; the woman stood toe to toe with Grant and didn't back down. That was an excellent quality to have, especially in business. He had to have the same quality to be successful in taking his company from start-up to multi-million dollar investments.

He was happy that the ceremony was over, and the reception was the only event remaining. Morgan would be turning over the day-to-day operations of this location to his youngest brother John. His brother was more than capable of taking the lead of the restoration and opening of their new hotel. With his hands off of this project, Morgan would be able to focus on other things, mainly Nurse Kyna.

"Erase that thought from your mind," Grant warned him.

"Whatever do you mean?" Morgan slapped his brother on the back and walked away, laughing. He hoped Grant didn't really see where his thoughts were going.

The reception for the groundbreaking went very well and was attended by several influential members of the business and local political world. Morgan mingled among the governor and the city's mayor. He also had the opportunity to speak with Raymond Conley, a multi-billionaire who lived in the area. However, Morgan's thoughts were never far from Kyna Hammond.

Later that day, Morgan retreated to the office in his hotel suite, to make a few business calls. One of those calls was to his personal assistant, Raven. She was hard-working, driven, and loyal – qualities he found lacking in the current workforce. He asked her to work some magic and find a phone number for Kyna. The tactic was a little underhanded, but he would deal with the potential fall-out later. Seeing her again was of the highest priority.

Morgan also needed to call "his guy" Carlton, who took care of problems for him. At the ceremony, a woman from Grant's past appeared and brought a truckload of drama with her. She was known for the spectacles she created, and whatever reason she was back couldn't be anything good.

Carlton handled delicate matters with discretion for Morgan. Keeping a clean image was most important to the Hawkins family, but dealing with other businessmen who thrived on underhandedness was problematic. Carlton was also paid handsomely for the work and results he produced.

Within an hour, Raven had a phone number for Kyna Hammond. Morgan hesitated after receiving the information and just stared at the phone number that was written on the notepad. He had no other choice but to take this route with her, since she change her phone number. Morgan tapped his pen against the desk and thought of the many scenarios that could play out, especially if Kyna was still angry. She could hang up the phone on him, or she could have calmed down and be willing to meet with him somewhere. He wouldn't know until he called.

The phone ringing seemed to go on forever, and Morgan was sure Kyna's voicemail was about to connect. Suddenly, a soft, demure voice answered.

"Hello?"

Morgan was silent, unable to speak. Her voice was sultry and not the angry sound from earlier.

"Hello?" she said a second time with a little aggravation.

"Sorry, this is Morgan?" he replied.

"And?" Kyna said sarcastically. That wasn't the response he expected, and it threw him off without a reply. She was intentionally being difficult.

"I...I...I...," he stammered before taking a deep breath to relax.

"What do you want?" she asked with an edge. Even her increasing anger was a turn-on for Morgan.

"I wanted to ask if you would join me for dinner or drinks." Morgan was finally able to gather his wits and ask.

There was a silent pause, and Morgan thought she may have ended the call. He was getting nervous, a feeling that he had not felt when asking a woman out on a date, ever.

"Tonight?" she softened her voice and asked.

"If you are available."

"I guess so. Where would you like to meet?"

Morgan smiled and felt his heart take a dip. He was inwardly excited; she had accepted his invitation—one point for him.

"I heard of a place called Crescendo's."

"I know the place. I'll meet you there in an hour," she responded dryly.

Morgan heard a soft click. She had ended the call with no further conversation. He figured it wouldn't be a good idea to make her wait and quickly changed into more comfortable clothing. Instead of the dark blue suit from earlier, he wore jeans, a crisp button-up shirt, and a grey blazer.

Crescendo was an intimate restaurant known for having live musical performances. He entered and immediately noticed the place wasn't crowded for a Friday evening. There was also a jazz saxophonist on stage performing. The maître D greeted Morgan and escorted him to a table in a secluded area as requested. From his seat, he would be able to see Kyna when she entered.

Morgan was thankful that the restaurant didn't allow smoking; that was one of his pet peeves. He took his health and the health of those around him very seriously. Every hotel or residential building the Hawkins Group renovated had a state-of-the-art gym accessible to its residents or guests. Morgan started his mornings with an intense two-hour workout, a minimum of three times a week. He would also spar at the boxing gym near his New York condo. Working out was essential to his physical and mental self-care.

*****

Kyna had come straight home after the ground-breaking ceremony. She needed to get caught up on her reading. She wanted to read a few medical journals and an article on new research around infertility she needed to study. Unfortunately, she was unable to concentrate on her reading. Seeing Morgan was unraveling her sense of control. She had not seen or talked to him since changing her phone number a few months ago.

She was dozing off and sleep overtook her when the ringing from her cell phone startled her awake. The caller-ID showed it was from the Hawkins Group, and Kyna knew it was Morgan. The phone rang, and she internally debated whether she should answer. Emotions she hadn't felt in quite some time had her confused. Before the voicemail could kick in, she quickly answered the phone.

His voice sent her over the edge. Only her stealthy resolve kept her true feelings in control. The invitation for dinner came at a much-needed time. She was ready for a break from reading. After she ended the call, Kyna raced to her closet to find something appropriate to wear.

Not wanting to encourage Morgan in any way, she decided to keep her attire simple. She chose a black skirt and a pink blouse for dinner. Not wanting to tempt him in any way, she was there just to get a free dinner and to get away from her house and work.

Crescendo was a newer restaurant on the other side of town and Kyna had always wanted to visit. The live music was also a plus for her. She loved the intimacy of smaller venues and the soulful sounds of jazz bands.

Upon her arrival, the valet parking attendant opened her door and greeted her, reaching for her hand to assist her from the car. She drove a red Toyota Camry, a graduation gift to herself from undergrad. It was old but clean and functional. Clutching her purse, she tugged on her skirt and strutted toward the restaurant's door.

The Maître D was a friend of hers. They talked for a short moment before he escorted her toward the rear of the restaurant. She used that time to get a hold of her racing pulse. Her nerves had flared up and was producing a nervous energy around her. She needed to remain calm.

Morgan was watching her approach and stood as she came closer. He was impeccably dressed in a tailor-made smoke grey jacket dressed down in jeans, just the way she liked him. Morgan was more than handsome. Kyna thought he was beautiful, with his perfectly trimmed goatee outlining his kissable lips.

"Hello, Mr. Hawkins," she greeted him, attempting to control her turbulent emotions.

Always the perfect gentleman, he gently grabbed her hand and pulled her close. "Good evening, Mrs. Hawkins."

Morgan placed a soft kiss to her temple and lingered above her for a few seconds. He then waited for her to be seated before returning to his chair.

"I like this place," she responded nonchalantly.

"I'm glad. I remembered you talking about coming here," Morgan cleared his throat. "I'm glad you came," he added after she didn't respond.

"Yeah, well, I'm not sure why I accepted your invitation. I'm not ready to give you an answer," Kyna fidgeted with her napkin.

"I'm not looking for an answer. I just want to have dinner with my beautiful wife." Morgan gently grabbed her hand and softly caressed her palm with his thumb. "Remember our first date?"

"Morgan, please don't do this," Kyna whispered. In just a few words, he was able to release the emotions she was miserably failing at hiding.

"Kyna, I miss you," he watched a tear escape her beautiful eyes. "I still love you...just like on our first date," Morgan kissed her tears away.

Kyna didn't want Morgan to know how much she remembered their first date – the date that led to their wedding day. When she remembered happier times, she would forget why they were estranged. The same evening, they had met by chance; he had come into town to meet with her sister, Poe, about purchasing a building for his new hotel.

Chapter 2 – From The Beginning

Kyna didn't know who Morgan was when they first met. He was just a handsome man sitting all alone at the bar in the hotel lobby. He seemed to be caught in his own world, having a drink when she entered with a couple of friends. They were celebrating her graduation from graduate school, getting her doctorate degree in nursing. More friends joined their small group after a few drinks, and now they were partying loudly. Soon, Kyna had everyone in the bar celebrating with her, except for the handsome man, brooding in the corner all alone. A few shots of tequila later had Kyna approaching the stranger.

"Hi! There is a party going on," she waved her hands in the direction of the party-goers.

"So I noticed," he responded, grimly taking another sip of his drink.

"Want to join us?" Kyna asked.

"I wouldn't be good company right now," he replied, never looking up from his glass.

Kyna, again, noticed how handsome he was. His goatee outlined a pair of the sexiest lips she had ever seen. Sadly, his golden-brown eyes seemed melancholy, and she wanted to cheer him up.

"Aww, honey. I think a party would be just the thing you need to turn that frown upside down into a smile."

Morgan raised his head and smirked at her corny joke.

"I got half a smile out of you. I'm winning," she smiled brightly. "Come on and join us."

"What are you celebrating?" Morgan asked, not making a move to leave his position.

"I just graduated with my doctorate degree in nursing. Three grueling years of research and writing," Kyna announced proudly.

"Congratulations, but I think I will pass. Enjoy the rest of your evening." He stood and motioned for the bartender, tossed a couple of bills on the bar and walked away.

Kyna felt sad for the stranger. There was something in his eyes that pulled her in, and she wanted to know more about what caused him to be gloomy. She brushed off his dismissal and rejoined her friends at the party. Her thoughts never far from him, and what would cause his sadness.

"Come on, girl, we don't need Mr. Stuffy Pants," Alexis wrapped her arm over Kyna's shoulder. "This is your party!"

Kyna continued to party for a while longer with her friends, but she couldn't stop thinking about the handsome stranger. The party crowd began to thin out, and Kyna decided it was time for her to call it a night and head to her room within the hotel. After a few hugs and kisses goodbye, she turned to her closest friends.

"Ladies, are we still on for brunch in the morning?" Kyna asked her friends, Alexis, Chelsea, Missy, and Nicola.

"If I wake up, I'll let you know," Alexis said, dangling a full shot glass in her hand.

"Don't worry, I'll make sure these drunk fools will be there," Chelsea added.

Chelsea, Alexis, and Kyna had been friends since grade school. With Kyna's sisters being older, she had to find friends her own age growing up. Her friends had always been there for her when her sisters couldn't. Missy and Nicola were friends from her days in undergrad. Kyna loved them all the same.

"Love you, girls. See you for brunch in the morning." Kyna hugged each one of them, grabbed her handbag, and headed toward her hotel room. Staying in the hotel made sense, seeing as Kyna knew she would be drinking and partying into the night. The next day would be a day of pampering in the hotel's spa.

The night was beautiful, with a clear sky and stars sparkling like diamonds. Kyna wanted to enjoy the night air and took a detour through the hotel's garden. She admired the flowers in bloom and how the moonlight reflected on their leaves. She took the time to inhale their fragrant scents as she leisurely walked by. Slowly, gliding through the roses, Kyna spotted her party pooper, sitting alone near the swimming pool. He was tall, over six feet, and he had broad shoulders. Kyna could tell he spent a lot of time working out. His muscles screamed through his suit jacket.

From behind a tall tree, she watched the stranger appear to be sulking in his own misery and staring off into space. He was a big guy but seemed so small at the moment. Kyna had an overwhelming feeling of wanting to be a friend for him. She decided to stop hiding and approach him.

"I was wondering how long you were going to stalk me," he asked as she approached.

"Stalk? No, I wasn't stalking you," she responded with a small laugh.

"What would you call it?" He looked up into her eyes, and Kyna melted just a little under his intense gaze.

"I was on my way to my room and noticed you sitting all alone."

"Like I said before, I wouldn't be good company right now," he lowered his head and stared into the pool.

"Let me be the judge of that. I'm a real good listener." Kyna took a seat in the lounger next to his and propped her feet up.

The moonlight reflected on his features, and she noticed he was more handsome than she initially thought. Suddenly, she sensed an unusual attraction to him, and she shook her head to get rid of the feeling.

"I promise, you don't want to hear any of this. It's just corporate business stuff."

"Oh, my favorite thing to talk about," Kyna smiled.

"You're funny. Well, I guess I could tell you. Unless you are a corporate spy from one of my competitors," Morgan joked with her. His smile made Kyna's stomach flip upside-down.

"Trust me, my favorite subject is obstetrics and reproductive therapy. Unless you have business interests in pharmaceuticals, I am of no worry to your business."

Morgan smiled and appeared to relax. Kyna got comfortable in her lounge chair and listened to him talk about the stress of running his business. She was shocked to learn that he owned several hotels and commercial properties in different cities and states. He spoke of things that went over her head, but she was able to keep up with the conversation for the most part.

She learned his name was Morgan Hawkins of the Hawkins Group, and he was in town to meet with a realtor about some properties he was interested in purchasing for developing a new hotel in the area.

"You know, my sister is the best realtor in town. If this guy you met with today doesn't work out, you should try the K. Hammond Realty Company."

Morgan laughed a deep belly laugh, and Kyna didn't know what was funny, but she laughed along with him. "What are we laughing at?" she asked.

"You and your sister have the same eyes."

Kyna sat straight up and looked at Morgan. Why would he say something like that, unless he knew her sister? "How would you know that my sister and I have the same eyes?"

"Because she is my realtor. A very professional and well-respected company, I might add."

Kyna relaxed and beamed as if the compliment was for her and not her sister. She loved her sisters with all her heart, and it pleased her to know that Morgan was using a small, local real estate company instead of a major broker.

They continued talking about random things, and after about an hour of listening to him talk, they both yawned at the same time.

"You know yawning is highly addictive," Kyna giggled.

There was a cleansing silence between the two of them as they just stared at each other. They both seemed to size the other up, not sure what to say or do next. Kyna wanted to listen to his deep soothing voice more but needed to get some sleep if she wanted to make it to brunch with her friends in the morning.

"How long will you be in the city?" Kyna asked.

"Why, you want to listen to more of my business ramblings?" Morgan joked.

"I enjoyed talking or rather listening to you." Kyna reached into her handbag and retrieved her business card. "Next time you are in town, give me a call. I like making new friends." Kyna gave him an exaggerated wink.

"Am I your friend now?" returning her smile and reaching for the card she offered.

"Only if you want to be," she flirted.

Kyna stood and offered Morgan her warmest smile. "I hope to hear from you soon." She walked away toward her room.

The next morning, while Kyna was getting ready to have brunch with her friends. Her thoughts were on her new friend Morgan, Mr. CEO. She hoped she might run into him on her way to the hotel's restaurant. Hopefully, their talk eased some of his stress. She might not have been able to assist him with any solutions, but maybe he was able to see things differently after speaking them out loud.

Chelsea and Alexis were sitting in the restaurant when Kyna arrived.

"Where are Missy and Nicola?"

"After you left last night, they decided that brunch was too bougie for them," Alexis answered, rolling her eyes upward. She never really liked Missy and only tolerated Nicola.

"They will not be joining us," Chelsea added.

"Honestly, Kyna, I don't know why you always invite them to everything. They don't seem to enjoy the things we do," Alexis said while reaching for a muffin in the basket at the center of their table,

"And, I am getting sick of them calling everything we do bougie," Chelsea grabbed her napkin and placed it in her lap.

"Fine, then we will just keep it the three amigas from now on, okay?" Kyna offered. She had no real intentions of discarding her friends, but she would try to keep the two groups away from one another.

"The way it should have been in the first place," Alexis tried to whisper under her breath.

Kyna adored her friends, but Alexis had an elitist attitude because she grew up wealthy, and Chelsea often followed

Alexis' lead. When she went to college and met new friends, Alexis all but accused her of replacing their friendship. Kyna tried to explain there was room for everyone in her life, but Alexis was jealous and showed it every chance she had.

The waiter appeared and took their drink and food orders. To keep with the celebration theme, the ladies had bottomless mimosas. Later in the afternoon, they had appointments for spa services to include facials, massages, manicures, and pedicures.

The friends talked about everything and nothing, just catching up with each other's lives. The last time the three of them had the time to get together was over six months ago. School kept Kyna busy for the past three years. Alexis was the Director of Nursing at a hospice facility, and Chelsea was a pharmacist, married with twin girls. Their lives were hectic.

The ladies had finished brunch and were ready to begin their spa treatments. Chelsea and Alexis argued over who would pay the bill for brunch when the waiter informed them that it had been settled.

"By who?" they asked in unison.

"He asked to remain anonymous," the waiter smiled and cleared a few plates from their table before walking away.

"Well, who am I to say no to a free meal?" Alexis laughed. Kyna smiled at her friends. They may be elitist or a little bougie, but they were hers and she loved them just the same.

Kyna looked around to see if Mr. CEO was somewhere nearby. She had a feeling he was responsible for paying for their brunch. That was something she thought he would do.

She was shocked again when they found out he had also taken care of everything for their spa services.

"Since I know I didn't meet anyone who could afford this kind of treatment last night," Chelsea pointed to herself. "And Alexis didn't meet anyone..." turning her attention to Kyna. "Who did you meet last night?"

"I talked with Mr. Stuffy Pants from the bar last night."

"You talked?" Alexis asked, not believing her.

"Just talked," Kyna remembered he talked, and she listened.

"Well, I don't know of any man to pay for all of this after just talking. So, keep your secrets," Chelsea told her, still not believing her. Kyna was also having a difficult time believing that Morgan would do all of this after just talking.

*****

Morgan noticed Kyna when she walked into the restaurant. She was just as he remembered her, beautiful and appearing carefree. Her excitement for her achievements made him feel happy for her, and he couldn't help but smile. She was young and had a goal, went after it, and crushed it in a short amount of time.

He may have done most of the talking last night, but he learned that she was 29-years-old and immediately knew she wanted to work in obstetrics from the beginning of her studies. She also had three older sisters whom she adored. Morgan felt a connection because he had three younger siblings that he felt the same way about.

He was also impressed with how focused she was at such a young age and how caring she was for others. She realized he didn't need to be alone and offered to just sit and listen to him talk about his stress. Most of the time, Morgan could tell she had no idea what he was talking about, but she never interrupted to ask questions. Kyna was a good listener, like she mentioned. And now, he had her phone number because she wanted to be friends. He wondered if she knew what kind of friends he wanted them to be.

The attraction was immediate from the first word in the bar, but Morgan had exercised control of his hormones and excused himself from her presence. Now, he watched her and her friends enjoy their brunch.

After waking that morning, Morgan decided that he would pay for her brunch as a graduation gift. But she deserved more; so on a whim, he paid for their entire spa treatment as well. Morgan was a giver; and had it not been for his siblings, he would probably give away all of his wealth. His siblings kept him grounded.

John was Morgan's youngest brother and a societal playboy. John had no problems sleeping with women from here to there. Leaving a trail of tears of his own making. Their mother would faint if she knew about the shenanigans John had been involved with. Melissa was their only sister and was more like a brother in some ways. She was rough and tough but had a feminine edge. Melissa would get down and dirty if she had to, then go get a manicure afterward. She was a sports fanatic in high school and was ultimately recruited by several schools for basketball and volleyball. She eventually chose a school known for business and not athletics. Their brother, Grant, was the prized son because he was a doctor. Not just any doctor, but a world-renowned obstetrician and gynecologist whose research in genetics and reproduction was being taught at many medical schools. Suddenly, a thought slapped Morgan across the face. Did Kyna and Grant know one another? She mentioned her field was obstetrics and reproduction. He quickly removed his phone from his jacket pocket and dialed his brother. What are the odds that Kyna's sister would be his realtor, and she would work with Grant? Unfortunately, his brother did not answer his phone. It was probably for the best because Morgan had no idea how he would ask the question without raising suspicion.

Morgan checked his calendar for his flight time. He was heading back to New York, where he had a condo and the home base for his company, before taking a mini-vacation in the islands. He needed a break, and after talking with Kyna, he needed that break right now.

After having his own brunch, he returned to his hotel suite and finished packing. Then, he called to have a bellboy retrieve his luggage. While he waited, his thoughts never strayed far from Kyna. He hoped she and her friends were enjoying themselves. He spared no expense and told the hotel manager they could have anything they wanted.

Later that afternoon, as Morgan was leaving the hotel to catch his flight, he stopped by the front desk to get a receipt and noticed that Kyna and her friends didn't spend nearly as much as he thought they would. She was becoming even more fascinating to him. His experience had been that women would take advantage of an open account for the spa. But, Kyna and her friends stayed conservative with their spending.

He laughed aloud, then turned and saw Kyna heading in his direction. She must have known he would be in the lobby because she marched right up to him, and his heart melted at her smile. An unknown feeling washed over his body. This was like nothing he had ever felt before.

"So, Mr. Moneybags," Kyna teased. "Thanks for everything, but it was unnecessary."

Morgan noticed how her hair flowed around her shoulders and created a beautiful silhouette framing her face. "It was a gift. A graduation gift. You deserved it," Morgan answered.

"Do you just go around paying the bill for women everywhere you go?" Kyna asked suspiciously.

"Not at all, but you were celebrating an accomplishment that few obtain. I hope you and your friends enjoyed yourselves."

"We did. Thank you very much." Morgan watched her scan him from head to toe, taking note of his tailor-made suit and expensive personalized cufflinks. He wondered if she was an opportunist or genuinely impressed by his attire. Nothing from their conversation the night before indicated she cared one way or another about his wealth. Even now, she was appreciative of his gift, but also humbled by the gesture.

"I also noticed you didn't spend nearly as much as I thought you would," Morgan stated, trying to get a response from her. Women in his circle usually spent thousands of dollars on hair and nails. He wondered if she was the same.

"Did you think I would go on a crazy spending spree? Sorry, not my style. Besides, I have my own money," she tossed the words over her shoulder as she turned and walked away.

What she said was notable, and he didn't know how to respond. She was unlike any woman he had ever met, aside from his sister and mother. He wanted to continue talking with her more than anything. She was intriguing and refreshing. Most women he came across were socialites of no substance, who only cared about how many followers they could get.

Morgan watched her walk away and smiled. *Friends.* That was what she said when she gave him her business card. He needed a friend like her.

Later that evening, once he made it safely home to New York, he sent his new friend a text message. She immediately responded. That surprised him. They held a quick text message conversation because she was at work. Morgan had not found out if she worked with or even knew his brother Grant. He couldn't figure out how to bring it up.

For the remainder of the week, Morgan was busy with meetings and conference calls, leaving him to only send quick text messages to Kyna here and there. He wished he could call her instead of messaging back and forth. Talking was much better than texting, in his opinion. Plus, listening to her talk was like hearing a soothing melody.

By Friday, they had discussed all types of subjects, from religion to politics to worldviews. He learned that she was the baby of her family and tended to dance to her own drumbeat. She hadn't told her family about her doctorate degree, fearing it would overshadow her sister's accomplishments.

Karleigh, her oldest sister, was preparing to get married, and Kaleigh was celebrating landing the Hawkins Group as a client, which was a significant deal for a small real estate firm like hers. Kyna didn't talk much about Karmyn, saying that her sister hid her true feelings very well.Morgan liked that Kyna was her own woman and not afraid to step out and try new things. She was adventurous and intelligent, loving and beautiful. She was exactly the type of woman he wanted in his life.

Not too long ago, Morgan had prayed that he would meet a woman that would challenge his thoughts and ideas. In his prayer, he asked God that she be nothing like the women he was currently subjected to in social settings. Well, God does answer prayers. And Morgan hoped he kept answering prayers when he jumped on his jet and headed back to see Kyna.

A week had passed since he last heard her voice, and it still sounded so sweet.

"Hi Kyna, it's your friend Morgan.

"Hi friend. how are you?"

"Happy that it's the weekend. Are you busy for the rest of the evening? I miss talking to you. My thumbs are getting tendinitis from all of the texting." He heard her laugh and relaxed. He also missed her laugh.

"I just left work. I guess I have time to talk."

"What about dinner? I'm in town and would love to see you."

Morgan felt a small amount of anxiety creep into his system. He hadn't thought about what would happen if she said no. He could simply ask her out for the next night, but what if she said no again. The fact that she still hadn't answered him was causing Morgan to get nervous.

"Sure, why not? I'm free. Where would you like to meet?"

Chapter 3

Morgan met Kyna at the Chateau Martinique, a French Caribbean fusion restaurant. He wanted their dinner to be uninterrupted and asked the manager for a private section near the rear. He also, discreetly, requested that no other patrons were seated at the tables near them and offered to pay for the privacy.

The restaurant's décor included lots of Caribbean-styled items, including fake palm trees and lots of straw coverings. Even the calypso music was adding to the ambiance. Kyna arrived right on time. Even in her tight-fitting jeans and a loose t-shirt, she still looked stunning. He wondered if he would have noticed her had she not been having a party in the hotel bar last week.

Kyna appeared self-assured and relaxed in his presence, which was different from the women he usually entertained. Other women were stuffy or too interested in materialistic things, like what type of car he drove or where he lived. Morgan once told a woman that he had three other roommates to help pay the bills. That woman left halfway through dinner. At least she didn't lie when she left; she simply told him things wouldn't work out between them.

"Would you like something to drink?" A glass of wine?" Morgan asked Kyna after she had been seated.

"No, thank you, just a glass of water. Do you drink a lot of wine?" she asked.

"Actually, I don't drink much at all. A glass of champagne every so often, but nothing heavy." Morgan preferred to be in control of his faculties at all times. He had seen enough drunkenness during college that he never wanted to be caught doing something stupid under the influence or wake up the next morning and not remember what happened the night before.

"Interesting, so what were you drinking at the bar last week?"

"That was tea... not Long Island, just straight sweet tea." Morgan stared at her, finding it hard to believe that she was real. No one woman had captured his attention for this length of time. Yet, she had him flying back across the country just to have dinner with her.

"Why are you looking at me like that?" she nervously looked down, then back up again. Before Morgan answered her, he stared into her eyes and drowned in their shape and color. She was so beautiful inside and out. Why hadn't he noticed her natural, long eyelashes? She batted them on occasion, and each time, he was mesmerized.

"You are different than the women I usually meet, and it's refreshing to talk to you. Not one time have you mentioned anything about how important your family is to society or how you can help benefit my business or social standing," Morgan honestly answered.

"Is that what women you date talk about?" Kyna laughed and tossed her hair back, revealing her slender neck. "That's so sad. No wonder you needed someone to talk to last week."

Morgan joined her in a good hearty laugh. He didn't care that a few people glanced in their direction. They didn't know the joy that he was having. He was excited to learn more about the enigma of this woman.

They talked for hours about their families and growing up with siblings. They shared stories about their years in college and the beginnings of their careers. She started school in Atlanta to major in psychology but decided to finish in an online nursing program. Morgan went to Howard University in Washington, D.C., for his undergraduate and graduate degrees in international business.

"So, tell me, Kyna, when was the last time you went on vacation? You seem to have been in school full-time for the past few years." Morgan asked, adding a little mystery to his question.

"I go on vacations, usually just weekend trips. I have the next two weeks off as a celebration to myself. I was planning to stay at a friend's cabin in the mountains. Just to have some peace and relaxation, catch up on some movies and tv shows. I'm heading that way tomorrow."

"I don't think I have watched TV or a movie in years," Morgan said more to himself.

"Really? What do you do to unwind and relax?"

He hadn't thought about relaxing in such a long time. Relaxing meant not attending to the many needs of his business. There were too many things that needed his attention within the company. John and Melissa could only handle so much, but he was the CEO and a bit of a control freak.

"I don't know. I don't think I have relaxed in a while," he replied.

"Well, it looks like you need a vacation more than I do. Let your brother and sister handle things at the company, take a break, and just relax."

She said it like it was something he could do without preparation. As if reading his thoughts, she added, "Your company will survive if you take a vacation." She winked at him.

Morgan thought more about her simple suggestion. John and Melissa had been begging him to take a break. Melissa often told him that he worked too much. There always seemed to be something that Morgan needed to attend to. He believed in his sibling's ability to handle things in his absence. But there was nothing like taking care of things on his own.

Melissa had proven her capabilities over time, and John was into having fun but could get the job done. Morgan was always serious about business when he needed to be, which seemed to be all the time. Maybe a vacation wasn't as far-fetched as he thought.

Kyna continued to talk about life, and they shared their personal goals, realizing they had more in common than he initially believed. With every word she spoke, Morgan felt a closer connection happening.

The restaurant began closing around them, but they continued to talk. The manager had agreed to stay open as long as they wanted him to after Morgan flashed his black card. The restaurant was now empty and Morgan realized the time was getting really late. He asked Kyna if she wanted to go for a walk; he wasn't ready to end the night.

The more they talked, the more Morgan felt connected to her. He had a feeling he may never find another woman like her in his lifetime. That crazy feeling of permanence had resurfaced a few times while they sat in the restaurant. She was becoming more than just a woman he liked talking to, but he was beginning to feel like he wanted to talk to her all the time.

They ended up walking along the waterfront and discussed current events, sports, and their previous relationships. Morgan didn't know how their conversation led to this particular topic, but he would use it to his advantage.

"Do you date often?" Morgan asked.

"Morgan, I've been in school nonstop for the past three years. I haven't had time to date," Kyna quickly answered.

That bit of information made his inside smile. He hadn't dated seriously in a few years, so they also had that in common. Kyna asked about his huge smile.

"I guess I'm glad that I am not stepping on another man's toes," Morgan grabbed her hand and immediately felt a charge through his arm. The feeling was a subtle but tingly jolt.

"You may have been stepping on another woman's toes," Kyna teased.

That statement caused Morgan to stop in his tracks. He never once got that vibe from her. But she was with a bunch of women last week at the bar. Maybe he was reading something that wasn't there.

Kyna laughed so hard she started crying. "If you could see your face right now. Calm down, I am not a lesbian."

Trying to save face, he replied, "that's okay if you were, I'm definitely one."

They both laughed at his attempt at a joke and continued walking in a comfortable, happy silence. Morgan thought Kyna had a beautiful smile and a great sense of humor. She was intelligent, driven, loved her family, and so much more. She was everything he ever hoped he would find in a companion. Not just a companion but a life partner.

The morning sun was peeking through the sky, and they had been together talking for the past 10 hours. Morgan had the craziest thought. They were so in tune with one another that he figured, why not ask. He walked over to an empty bench facing the water and sat down. Then patted the space beside him for Kyna to sit down. They watched the sun cross the horizon in silence.

"Kyna, this is going to sound crazy, but I feel something very different for you. Something that I have never felt for another woman. I am attracted to you, and my attraction is stronger than any physical attraction. I don't think I would ever tire of talking to you." He took both of her hands into his and gazed directly into her face. Taking a deep breath, he continued, "You can call me crazy, but I don't want this to end. Come with me to Vegas."

"Vegas?"

"Yes. I just want to spend more time with you. You will have your own room if that concerns you."

Morgan had not realized he was holding his breath again, waiting for her answer until she agreed. He let out a small sigh and looked into the opening sky, then silently said, "thank you."

*****

Kyna was really enjoying herself with Morgan. Before meeting him, she would have said all billionaire CEO's were uptight, stuffy, and megalomaniacs. Morgan was the exact opposite; he was funny, charming and down-to-earth. When he told her stories about growing up the oldest of four, he was endearing, and she could see that he loved his family. He wasn't just a billionaire; he was normal.

Conversing with Morgan was effortless. It had been a long time since Kyna was able to talk about her life goals with anyone without getting their opinion on what they thought she should do. Her sisters would support and encourage her if she wanted to be a clown in the circus, but her friends were different. They thought some of her dreams were unrealistic and unobtainable. That was until she achieved her goals, then they were encouraging. Morgan listened to her talk about her dreams, and not once did he appear to not believe in her. He asked her questions and provided suggestions to give her better clarity and insight into her decisions. Those moments were invaluable.

Tey continued talking until the restaurant closed, then they walked to the waterfront and talked some more. Kyna felt like she was catching up with a long–lost friend instead of a man she had just met the previous week. Talking with Morgan was easy and fun.

She could see in his eyes that he was struggling with his attraction to her. Kyna wondered if he could see her attraction to him reflected in her eyes. There was something akin to a magnetic force pulling them together. Even through the text messages, she felt drawn to him. Those quick text messages were better than some conversations she had on past dates.

Everything about Morgan was seemed perfect. Kyna knew that he had his flaws, but they seemed minor. Morgan worked himself in knots; he rarely rested or took vacations, and he could be ruthless in business dealings by his own admission. But his caring and giving spirit overshadowed all of his flaws.

Last night, she prayed that Morgan was the real deal and not some rich guy just trying to slum with the normals in middle-class America. She asked God to show her the real Morgan. Then, out of nowhere, he was in town asking her to dinner. Was this luck or divine intervention?

Kyna wanted to kiss him, hug him, feel his arms around her body. The more he talked, the more his velvet voice wrapped around her heart. She pondered if this was how love at first sight felt. The initial attraction she felt was between their minds, then something else happened - a click. She felt the pit of her stomach fall like the drops on a roller coaster.

When he asked her to go to Vegas, she only hesitated so that she didn't appear too eager. She had never been to Vegas. Her grandmother called it Sin City, but Kyna wanted to see the magnificent hotels and try all of the casino buffets. She didn't gamble, but the nightlife could be exciting, and maybe they could take in a show or two. Vegas sounded much better than being alone in the mountains.

But when he asked her the next question, Kyna's mouth dropped and nothing came out. She was shocked beyond belief.

"I am asking if you will marry me? I know this sounds crazy, but I can't seem to want you out of my life. We are so connected in ways I never knew existed. I think this is what love feels like. A love that I have never felt before. And now I can't stop rambling," he laughed.

Kyna thought even his laugh sounded good, and she wanted to hear it more. The crazy feeling she was having was telling her to say yes. She had to admit that she toyed around with the feeling of love too. All week they had sent text after text. She thought he was too good to be true. A chance meeting in a hotel bar leading to this was unheard of. What kind of Hallmark movie did she walk into?

"Morgan, is it crazy that I want to say yes? But, are you sure? Really sure?"

He didn't immediately answer, and that caused Kyna to unconsciously hold her breath. If he answered yes, then she was accepting his proposal. But, instead of answering right away, he took her hands in his, held them tightly, and gazed into her eyes.

After several seconds that felt like minutes, he answered, "I love the Lord with all of my heart. Those aren't just words; that is the foundation for my life. There is no greater love than the love of the Lord. I wake every morning and pray. And every evening, I thank God for another day." He paused again, seeming to gather his thoughts before speaking. "I prayed for a woman just like you. Proverbs 18:22 says He who finds a wife finds a good thing and obtains favor from the Lord. With you, I have found favor. And, if you say yes, I know God's love continues to pour down on me."

Morgan kissed her hands and then used his thumb to wipe away the tears that flowed down her face. She couldn't believe that this man she had just met last week was asking her to marry him and she was accepting his proposal.

"What are you doing this weekend?" he laughed, pulling her into his strong embrace.

"Morgan, are you crazy? I can't get married this weekend. My parents will never approve of us marrying so soon. We will need to date more and plan a proper wedding."

"Kyna, let's get married tonight. Let's go to Vegas and later plan a wedding for our families. I can't let you walk away from me and not be my wife."

"I think we are both crazy, but okay," she whispered. She had no idea what she was doing, but her adventurous side was ready to follow Morgan anywhere he led.

Morgan grabbed her around the waist and twirled her around before gently setting her back onto her feet. Nothing seemed real even as Morgan started calling people. First, he contacted his pilot to prepare for them to go to Vegas within the hour. Then he called his personal assistant, who seemed to be awake this early in the morning on a Saturday.

Morgan wouldn't let Kyna stop by her apartment to pack anything. Instead, he told her he would buy her everything she would need. The jet was airborne, and Morgan was still talking to someone on the phone. It was close to 8 A.M., Kyna thought it was a good thing her family thought she was heading to the mountains for rest and relaxation, or she would have to explain why she missed church and Sunday dinner.

Kyna started thinking about her sisters. What would they think if she told them? They would definitely try talking her out of getting married. Especially Karmyn, who had been married to her college sweetheart and is now divorced. Kyna knew the subject of marriage was a tough subject for Karmyn to discuss.

This wasn't what she envisioned her wedding day to be. Kyna dreamed of having a Cinderella-themed wedding, with the horse-drawn carriage and everything. Morgan promised he would give her a dream wedding when they had time to plan it properly. Her heart kept plummeting, and it had nothing to do with her flying on a private jet. She was really doing this. She was going to Vegas to get married. And when she looked to her future husband, and he smiled at her, she felt she was doing the right thing.

Kyna nodded off during the flight and was nudged awake as they were preparing to land in Las Vegas. "Wake up, beautiful. We are about to land. Kyna, have you ever been to Vegas?"

"No, I don't gamble," she answered, groggily coming awake.

Morgan laughed, "There is more than just gambling. There are great shows and food in some of these casinos."

"So I've heard. I can't wait to check out those buffets," Kyna looked out the window. The sun was just rising in the Pacific time zone, and the lights were still visible from the strip where most of the casinos were located.

"Kyna, are you sure about this? I know I'm sure, but I want to make sure you are not feeling pressured, or if you are having doubts, let me know," Morgan rambled. Kyna realized he did that when he was nervous.

"No doubts," she returned his smile.

"I have one more request." He held her hand to reassure her when he saw her smile falter. "Anything we face, we will face together. But, can we keep this between us for a while. I don't want to share you with anyone just yet."

Kyna felt like he was reading her mind. She was feeling the same way. If her family found out, they would try to declare her legally insane. Besides, she loved hearing him say he wanted them to enjoy marriage together, alone. That made every crazy thought she was having disappear.

"I agree. Let's be selfish and keep this between us. For a little while, anyway."

Once they landed, Morgan gathered her in his arms and just held her until they reached the private terminal. She loved the feel of his muscular arms wrapped around her, protecting her from the unknown, a simple gesture of his love. They taxied to a private terminal and were whisked away in a private car. Kyna wondered why he hadn't tried to kiss her yet. It seemed the next logical thing to do. She kept turning her face up to his, but he was a full foot taller than her, and maybe he wasn't getting the hint. Then, all of a sudden, she thought of her wedding night. She was a virgin and, until now, had not considered what he would think about her inexperience.

"Are you okay, baby? You started shivering," Morgan used his hands to rub her arms up and down, attempting to warm her.

That was the first time he used any type of endearment when speaking to her. Up until then, it had always been "Kyna." She felt comfortable with him calling her "*baby*." His smooth voice actually calmed her down and made her remember what he said...They would work out anything they faced. She hoped that included her bedroom inexperience.

"I'm fine. Just a little tired."

Kyna marveled at the bright lights on the buildings, even visible in the daylight, before arriving at Caesars Palace. Morgan had secured a two-bedroom suite that allowed them to be separated while preparing for their wedding. The hotel was very accommodating at 8 o'clock in the morning. But Kyna figured they were used to this type of thing. Wealthy businessmen arriving at odd hours and demanding certain services.

Morgan was very attentive and had every detail planned. When she entered her room, there was a small assortment of fruits, muffins, coffee, and teas. On the bed was a printed tentative schedule of events. The schedule had her viewing dresses and accessories early, then getting some rest until the makeup and hairstylist arrived at 3 P.M.

Within the hour of arriving, a woman entered her suite with an armful of dresses for Kyna to choose from. Each dress had accompanying jewelry and shoes. The woman explained that all of the items were interchangeable.

"Honey, listen, if these dresses are not your style, I'll have someone deliver more choices. That man of yours is something special," Helen, who turned out to be the owner of a premier wedding dress boutique, gushed.

After selecting her wedding dress, jewelry, undergarments, and shoes, Kyna was able to rest before preparations began. The wedding was to start at 7:11 P.M. The time was the date of her birthday, July 11th. That little detail made Kyna love

Morgan more. She fell asleep as soon as her head hit the pillow, knowing she only had about four hours before she needed to wake.

For over an hour, the make-up artist and hairstylist made Kyna look beautiful for her wedding day. She screamed on the inside as the women transformed her into a glamorous girl. Everything happening was unbelievable. She was getting married!

Helen made alterations and returned her gown, a beautiful silk sheath dress in an off-white, with a flowing organza skirt decorated in Swarovski crystals. It was a perfect fit for her size four frame. Kyna was thin but toned, and happy that her years of yoga and Pilates would be visible through her dress.

At 7 P.M., Kyna opened the doors and stepped out into the living area. There, she first noticed Morgan dressed in a designer tuxedo and looking absolutely yummy. She almost missed seeing the suite had been decorated for the wedding. The room's furniture had all been moved to the side, and white and yellow roses were everywhere. There was an arch, also decorated with white and yellow roses. Kyna wanted to cry because Morgan had really listened to her when she talked about her favorite flowers and colors.

Other than Morgan, there were six other people in the room. Helen, her hairstylist, and makeup artist, remained for the ceremony. Two men dressed in the hotel's uniform and another man, she assumed, was the minister waiting under the arch. Her heart had that sinking feeling again, then Morgan stood in front of her, and the anxiety and fears were washed away. A peace washed over her. She knew in her heart, this was the right decision.

"You are absolutely gorgeous," Morgan lowered his voice, blanketing her with his warmth. The way he stared at her, the love he was sending her through his eyes, was enough to cause her heart to race again for an entirely different reason.

"Are you two ready?" the minister asked.

"Yes," they answered in unison.

"Heavenly Father, we are gathered here to join this man and this woman in holy matrimony. Instead of traditional vows, they will speak to one another."

"Ladies first," Morgan whispered.

"When we first met, I felt compelled to be there for you. You seemed sad, like you needed a friend, and I wanted to be that friend. What I didn't know is that you would be my better half and that I would fall in love with you so fast. I want to be more than your wife. I want to be your best friend, lover, mother to your children, and life mate forever. I love you, Morgan Hawkins, today and forever."

"There is so much more we must learn about one another, but there is no one else I want to go through this life with other than you. God touched my heart and told me you were for me the first time we talked. With everything I have, you will want for nothing. I promise to love you beyond measure, and I am blessed to be your husband."

By the end of their vows, everyone in the room was in tears, including the two men from the hotel staff. Kyna barely noticed the others because she was crying at the sight of the ring Morgan was sliding onto her finger. The center diamond was huge. If she had to guess, maybe it was three or four carats. The band was a double ring of smaller princess cut diamonds. This ring would bring attention for sure.

"By the powers invested in me, by the state of Nevada, in front of these witnesses and before God, I now pronounce you husband and wife. You may kiss your bride," the minister said.

Morgan stared at Kyna, not kissing her and not saying anything. Kyna was getting extremely nervous, then Morgan leaned in and whispered, "I love you," against her lips before kissing her and deepening the kiss for several seconds while their guest cheered.

Kyna heard a champagne cork pop in the background, but the look Morgan was giving her drowned out everyone in the room.

The newly wedded couple began their marriage with a private dinner on the balcony of their suite. The two hotel employees were the chef and server for their dinner. Morgan remembered she loved Italian food and all things spicy. For dinner, she was served penne alla'arrabbiata and a side salad. Morgan was eating his favorite, fried chicken and sweet potato fries. For dessert, the hotel provided them with individual miniature wedding cakes. Both were chocolate, their favorite flavor, something else they shared.

"How did you find a minister available so quickly?" Kyna asked, popping a strawberry into her mouth.

"I have a great personal assistant. Raven has been my right arm for a few years."

"Is she pretty?"

"Ah, do I have a jealous wife?" Morgan teased her but got serious when he noticed Kyna wasn't laughing. "She is beautiful, but she is also married with four adorable children. You, my gorgeous wife, have nothing to worry about."

Kyna visibly relaxed. Her brief moment of jealousy was a reflex. She had been lied to before by men, but she trusted Morgan. She believed Morgan loved her beyond doubt. The green-eyed monster would have to be put to rest.

"So, will our honeymoon be here in Vegas?" Kyna asked, trying to get a hint from him.

"No. That, my dear, is a surprise. Raven is working out the details, and you will get to meet her soon. She is flying out here so I can sign some papers, and then we are free to move about the planet."

They had previously talked about Kyna's plans to spend the week relaxing in the mountains, but she was hopeful that they were going somewhere else for their honeymoon. Writing her dissertation and then defending it was a stressful nine months, and she needed to be away from everything and everyone.

Kyna had been studying for her doctorate without her family's knowledge. Getting this degree was something she wanted for herself, but also as a surprise to her parents. Her family assumed that being a nurse was her end goal. When she returned to school for her master's degree, her father thought it was because she needed more education to move forward in her career. Really, the master's degree was the foundation for continuing to her real goal.

After dinner, Kyna became nervous about what would happen next. Helen had her purchase several items from a lingerie shop. They arrived, wrapped in individual white boxes. Each item was dainty and lacy, and she only had to keep what she wanted and return the rest.

"Baby, talk to me. You just got quiet. We've been talking to each other for the past 24 hours. I want us to continue to build on our marriage, with trust and honesty. I can see it in your eyes that you are worried about something. Tell me what it is?" Morgan gently grabbed her hand and used his thumb to trace circles in the palm of her hand.

"Morgan, I don't want to be a disappointment to you. I'm not experienced in the bedroom," Kyna shyly ducked her head, averting eye contact.

"Is that all?" he laughed. "You can never disappoint me. What you don't know, I'll teach you."

He leaned for a kiss, and if it were possible, this kiss was softer and more gentle than the first kiss they shared when they said, "I do." How can a man, so big and strong, have the most delicate lips, she wondered?

Their intimate moment was interrupted by a knock on the door.

"Don't go anywhere; that must be Raven."

Raven Alvarez was indeed beautiful. Her skin was a smooth golden bronze, and her eyes were a brown hazel. Her jet-black hair reached her waist and was fastened into a tight ponytail at the nape of her neck. When she noticed Kyna sitting on the balcony, she brushed past Morgan and headed straight for her.

"Congratulations, Mrs. Hawkins! I'm Raven, and I'm here to serve you as well. Anything you need, just call me." She handed Kyna a business card with her contact information. "Pardon me for saying, but you are stunning. I'm sorry to keep staring at you, but you are exactly what I pictured for Mr. Hawkins."

Kyna smiled and fell in love with her husband's personal assistant. "Thank you."

"I'm sorry for rambling on. I'm just so excited for you two. If Morgan didn't tell you, I am a sucker for romance. I've been married for 15 years, and my husband still sends me flowers every week."

Raven kept talking and gushing over Kyna. She barely paid any attention to Morgan as he slipped the documents from her hands and left the two ladies to talk. He returned a few minutes later.

"Alright, Raven, you and I have some business to discuss. Kyna, this won't take long," Morgan nudged Raven.

"Yes, we do. Oh, Kyna, it was a pleasure to meet you. I hope we can do lunch in New York soon."

"It was a pleasure to meet you, as well. Thank you for everything."

Morgan and Raven went into the suite to discuss business while Kyna relaxed on the balcony. She hadn't realized she had fallen asleep until she felt those soft lips on hers.

"Wake up, sleepyhead."

"How long was I asleep?" she drowsily asked.

"About an hour. Come on, baby, we need to do some shopping before we leave for our next destination. Raven had a few stores reopen just for us."

Kyna was hesitant, and it must have shown on her face. Morgan turned to her and asked, "What's wrong, baby?"

"I don't know how to ask this?" She fidgeted with her hands.

"Just say it."

Kyna kept her eyes staring downward as she asked, "When are we going to consummate our marriage?"

Morgan pulled her into his embrace, forcing her to look up. He smiled and just stared at her. She felt safe in his arms, but he wasn't answering her question, and she wanted to know.

"Kyna, when we make love, I want it to be perfect, just like you. It's our wedding day, but our wedding night will be filled with passion." He kissed her down one side of her neck to the other and ended on a passion–filled lip lock. This kiss was different from their "I do" kiss. This one promised she would not be disappointed in the bedroom.

Kyna was in heaven as Morgan took her to several stores in Caesars Palace to shop for anything she wanted. Just past 11 P.M., and the stores opened just for Morgan. She wasn't used to this type of wealth and frequently frowned at the prices of some items.

"Ain't no way I'm paying $600 for these shoes," Kyna said, placing the Salvatore Ferragamo sandals back on the table.

"Baby, I'm paying for the shoes, and if you want them, get the shoes. You are Mrs. Hawkins now. Remember, you are worth billions."

Kyna wasn't sure how to feel when he said billions. Of course, she knew he was a billionaire, and they had previously discussed whether or not to have a pre-nuptial agreement. Morgan was adamantly against it. He said that those agreements were for people who weren't sure if they really loved one another. He was confident about his love for Kyna, and he promised himself when he got married, he would never have one.

They continued shopping, with Kyna purchasing all of the necessary items she would need for a week away from home. Especially since her husband wouldn't let her go home to pack anything. All she had was the overnight bag she kept in her car for the nights when she worked late at the hospital.

Chapter 4

For the second time in 24 hours, they were boarding a jet to begin their honeymoon. Kyna wanted to know the location, but Morgan was keeping a tight lip. Even the pilot and flight attendant were staying quiet. She knew it was someplace tropical because Morgan made sure she purchased several swimsuits, sandals, and sundresses.

Being wined, dined, and flown to unknown parts of the world on a private jet was not how Kyna expected her week to begin, but she enjoyed every minute of it. They had been in the air for over an hour, and Morgan still had not told her where they were going. He was secretive about everything, and strangely, Kyna was enjoying the surprises.

Kyna was admiring the view of the earth from her window. The mountain ranges were breath-taking. "Morgan, I feel like I'm dreaming. So much has happened in the past three days. I feel like Cinderella."

"This is very much real. We will be arriving soon. Are you ready?"

"Ready for what? I wish I knew where we were going," she asked coyly.

Morgan stopped reviewing his documents and placed them in his briefcase. He smiled before answering her, "I guess I could tell you since we are almost there. Soon we will be enjoying the sandy beaches of Cabo San Lucas."

Kyna jumped up and squealed, "We're going to Cabo? I've never been there! Oh my God!" She plopped in Morgan's lap and peppered him with kisses. He tightened his hold on her and returned her kisses. Their kissing fest was interrupted by the pilot announcing they were approaching their destination and preparing for landing.

There was a limousine waiting at the private airport that drove them to their remote cottage in a gated community right on the beach. Kyna tried to take in the sights as they passed resort after resort. The sun was rising over the horizon, and the beach was perfectly still. She could see the waves from the Pacific Ocean gently crashing against the shore.

Their cottage was vast and spacious. Much larger than her apartment. Kyna thought there was too much space for one couple to need. She loved the floor-to-ceiling wall of windows that faced the ocean and the large chef's kitchen that also overlooked the beach.

Kyna stepped out onto the balcony and smelled the morning air. The sounds of the crashing waves against the sand were calming to her senses. Her life was too good to be true.

*****

Morgan was silently thanking God for sending Kyna into his life. He wouldn't tell her this, but he had been sulking the night they met because he had no one special to share his good news with. He was about to build a boutique hotel, which was something he always wanted to do. A small quaint resort where people would stay and truly relax. Yet, he had no special someone in his life to share that with.

While he waited for their luggage to be brought inside, he watched Kyna go from room to room. Her excitement amused him. It had been a long time since he kept company with someone who appreciated their surroundings and the simple things in life. She seemed to stop at every painting and touched the sofa's fabric and the chairs before opening the doors to the patio.

After tipping the valet, Morgan quietly watched his wife standing on the balcony, enjoying life. He joined her and wrapped his arms around her waist. Her scent was so unique to her, and he could inhale her presence all day. They stood on the balcony in silence for several minutes.

"Hello, beautiful." Morgan kissed the side of her neck. "We will be here for a week; let's go get settled in and unpack our luggage. Maybe we can go for a tour later."

"Okay," she turned to face him, placing her arms around his neck. "My heart is full. I love you so much."

"I'm glad to hear that." Morgan took Kyna by the hand and led her into the cottage. They walked past the all-white sofa in the living room and into their large bedroom for the week.

"I think my apartment can fit in this bedroom alone."

"Kyna, if you want a bigger place, let me know. I meant what I said, anything you want, within my power you will have."

That put a smile on her face that he loved to see.

Their bedroom had more wall-to-ceiling windows with magnificent views of the ocean. Morgan watched Kyna walk around and observe every detail. The room had two wardrobes to either side of the bed. Kyna started taking her newly purchased items from her suitcase and placed them in the wardrobe.

They took a few minutes to empty their luggage. When Morgan turned to check on Kyna's progress, he had the shock of his life.

She was standing next to the bed, wearing all-white silk lingerie. His jaw fell to the floor, but only for a moment. Just like he imagined, her body was flawless. Morgan thought she appeared angelic and pure and all his. He stalked toward her, never losing eye contact. Her passion simmering in the way she returned his stare. He wanted to ask her if she was ready, but he wasn't sure if he was ready for what comes next.

"Lord, help me."

Their first full day as a married couple would be perfect, just like her.

*****

The next morning, Morgan awakened with the rising sun, feeling refreshed and renewed. He had always been an early riser and whole-heartedly believed that the early bird caught the worm. Trying not to wake his sleeping beauty, he eased out of bed to find his cell phone. He wanted to check his emails. Raven had updated his out-of-office response for those few people that had his personal email address. All other emails were rerouted back to Raven.

"Baby, you promised, no work this week," Kyna sleepily whispered.

Morgan tossed the phone onto the nightstand, "You're right. No work." He rolled over closer to her to begin another session of love thy wife.

Chapter 5

After a week of sunshine, beaches, long talks and longer steamy nights, Kyna and Morgan had to return to their real lives. Neither wanted to discuss how life after the wedding would look. Their first week of marriage had met every one of Kyna's dreams.

They started each day in prayer and then took long walks along the beach. After breakfast, there was a day full of activities. Morgan taught her how to snorkel and scuba dive. He wanted to teach her to fish, but she adamantly refused. Holding a live fish was not something she found fun.

One day they rode ATV's along the beach and in the desert. Kyna had never seen so many cacti in her life. She cherished the time they spent together, learning more about one another. When she thought about how they rushed into marriage, it was their time getting to know each other, which made her smile. Talk about putting the cart before the horse.

However, during their week together, they had avoided talking about what comes next after the honeymoon. On the flight home, they had no choice but to discuss the changes to their new lives together.

"We will be in the air for the next 5 hours. I think it's time we address the elephant in the room," Morgan started the conversation like he would a board meeting. He was straight to the point.

Snuggled closely with Morgan, Kyna giggled, "I was just imagining an elephant on this jet."

Morgan smiled, but tried to remain serious, "Kyna, we need to talk."

"I know," she moved from his side and sat in the chair across from him. "This is the part we didn't really think all the way through." Kyna had told him about the research project she was working on with his brother Grant. They had applied for grants and were awaiting notification. "My job and the work I do are very important to me. I can't leave the hospital."

"Baby, I would never ask you to leave your career. So, I have some ideas. I had my security guy check out your apartment and it is not secure enough for us."

Kyna interrupted Morgan, "Wait, your security guy was at my apartment? When? And what do you mean by not secure?" Kyna sat back in her chair, stiffening her spine. She wasn't sure how she felt about Morgan taking it upon himself to do a security inspection on her apartment.

"Kyna, that ring on your finger is worth $30,000. Since we are not telling people about us yet, I figured you would want to leave it at home. Your apartment is too vulnerable to break-ins."

She wanted to argue with his assessment but couldn't. Her apartment was in a good neighborhood, but even the best neighborhoods were susceptible to home invasions. Still, she wasn't ready to give in just yet. She was thinking of a snappy comeback when he continued talking.

"I was also thinking of buying you a condo in the medical district, near my brothers John and Grant. It's an up-and-coming area, gated community and near the hospital." When she didn't appear to reject the idea, he continued, "I will have a top-notch security system put into place. The condo also allows us the privacy we need."

She listened to everything he had to say, and it was evident that her security and safety were his primary concerns. Kyna loved her apartment; she had lived there since graduating from college. Her very first place, all to herself. Now, she was being asked to give it up.

Kyna wasn't sure why getting a new place felt like she had to depend on someone to take care of her again. When she lived at home with her parents and then on campus, her parents paid her bills. They also told her what she could do and who she could invite over. Since being on her own, she had the freedom she cherished.

Instead of voicing her concerns with Morgan, she asked, "Are you planning to move your headquarters?"

"No, I will continue to work from New York, but I want to be with you for every day off you have. Make sure Raven has your schedule, and she will make the arrangements for me to be with you or for you to come to me." Kyna was getting irritated by Morgan continuing to use his boardroom voice. This wasn't some acquisition and merger; this was her life, their life.

"I work four days on and four days off on a normal weekly rotation. Then, there are the women in our trial who could go into labor at any time. I have to be available to them." Kyna informed him. He hadn't noticed she turned her gaze away from him to stare out of the window.

"If you need to go to work when I'm there, then you go. I understand how your work is important to you. Kyna, I don't want to disrupt your life in any way. But we are married now, and until we tell the world, we have to do things a little differently now."

She knew he was right. Deep down in her spirit, she felt everything he was doing was for their future. With a deep sigh, she turned to him and said, "Morgan, I don't know how I got so blessed to marry a man like you. I love you so much."

"I take it you like these ideas," Morgan flashed her that mega-watt smile that made her feel gooey on the inside. When he looked at her that way, she would agree to almost anything.

"Yes, they are perfect. However, I do want to keep my apartment for a little while. My sisters would become suspicious if I were to suddenly move out. I promise to keep my jewelry and these expensive Jimmy Choo shoes at the condo under lock and key."

Again, Morgan laughed and Kyna thought of all the fun and laughter they did over the past week. She loved everything about this man; and to make the deal sweeter, he was a man of God. Her parents would love him for that reason alone.

"I also want you to have access to all of my properties. I never told you about all of them. A set of keys will be delivered to your apartment. I have a home in New York and Miami. I share a condo with a business associate in Chicago, Seattle, and LA," Morgan continued speaking.

"You have five homes?" Kyna asked, astonished.

"I do lots of business in those areas. And, my siblings and I have a house in the Turks and Caicos."

"Your wealth is larger than I thought," Kyna said under her breath, hoping he didn't hear her. But, he did.

"Our wealth," he corrected her. Moving closer to her, he grabbed her hands in his and held them firmly. "You are my wife. What I own, you own. You have to accept that you are now the billionaire's wife."

Kyna was working on accepting her new role. But just because she married him and he was wealthy didn't automatically mean she was too. At least not her mind. She didn't marry Morgan because of his wealth, and she wasn't going to go crazy with spending just because she could.

She gave Morgan a reassuring smile, giving him the go-ahead to continue. She could tell he had more to say.

"Baby, I also took the liberty of paying off all of your debt."

Kyna jumped out of her chair, stared at him incredulously and then sat down before standing again. "All of it?"

"Yes, student loans, car payment, and credit card. I'm actually shocked you only had one credit card," Morgan laughed.

"I'm not going to ask how you got that information." She plopped back down into her seat. Not only was her husband wealthy, but he was very resourceful. She was appreciative that he had taken care of her debt that way, but she was starting to feel like a child again. Always having her parents to take care of her. "I am extremely grateful that you did that, but you didn't have to. I have a nice paying job."

"Now you can take your money from your *nice paying job* and do anything you want. Bills will not be one of them," he said that with finality to his words. They would not discuss bills or debt again.

They continued to talk more about the logistics and privacy needed surrounding the secrecy of their marriage. Morgan wanted to wait a year before telling anyone what they had done. Both sets of parents would be upset, but Kyna kept thinking about her sisters. She didn't know how they would react to her being married.

Growing up, her sisters always treated her like a child. Even in her adult years, she was their baby sister. Their treatment was part of the reason Kyna kept her distance from them now. She loved her sisters to no end and would fight for them if she had to, but she wasn't as close to them as they were with each other.

*****

Morgan contacted Raven while they were still in flight. He had already started the process of purchasing the condo and acquiring a security system for her current apartment. He didn't think she would agree so fast, but he was hopeful that she would. In the end, she only wanted to keep her apartment, which made perfect sense. There was no need to draw any attention to her by moving apartments without any provocation.

He realized he was throwing a lot of information at her. Last week, she had no idea who he was and now they were married. Morgan had to tell himself that this was his life and not a business transaction. He caught himself a couple of times speaking to her like she was a business partner. When she glared out the window, he knew she was thinking hard about something.

This entire whirlwind romance they had was coming to an end, and she had to have been feeling something. Morgan admitted that he was getting nervous about leaving her. What if she decided she had made a mistake? What if she was after his money and wiped him clean? He dismissed that last thought from his mind. Morgan had to force her to wear the Jimmy Choo's he purchased for her.

In time, they would figure things out, at least for the next year. If only he could wait that long.

Once the jet landed, he had a car service to meet them at the private airport.

"My wife, I love you," he stared deeply into her eyes. He wanted her to feel his love.

She returned his loving gaze with one of her own. "And I love you, but I know this is where we say goodbye."

"Not goodbye, but see you later. I will be back on Thursday night. And if you can, I want to take you away for the weekend."

"We just came back from a wonderful week in Cabo. Where are we going now?"

"To our home in Miami." She smiled when he said "our home." Morgan was going out of his way to make sure she understood they were in this marriage together and everything he had, she also had.

"Let me check my schedule and I will let you know."

The pilot opened the door and lowered the stairs. Now the two of them stood there, in the doorway, not wanting to let the other go.

"I will call you when I arrive in New York. If you need anything, call me. If you can't reach me, call Raven. She is available to you 24/7," Morgan instructed her.

Morgan left her with a passionate kiss and then a soft kiss to her temple. He watched her walk away and enter the vehicle. The car disappeared onto the road, and he felt his heart crumbling piece by piece. He had to remind himself that this was temporary and that he would see her again in a few days.

A few hours later, he arrived in New York and immediately had Raven on the phone.

"I'm back in the city; schedule an appointment with Carlton first thing Monday morning. Make sure to permanently move my weekly president's meeting to Wednesdays. Then arrange for the jet to take me to Kyna this Thursday and have us depart for Miami on Friday morning, returning on Sunday."

"Sure thing," Raven responded.

Morgan needed to take care of a few personal items and some business matters before leaving again for the weekend. He was also trying to think of a reason he could tell his sister, Melissa, why he was leaving town again. She was Vice President of Operations for the Hawkins Group and she would know if he were lying.

The Hawkins Group headquarters was located in New York City, but Morgan looked into other areas for a second headquarters. New York was losing the appeal it once had. Even before Kyna came into his life, he was ready to move on.

After ending his call with Raven, he immediately called Kyna and got her voicemail. He left a message and sent her a brief text letting her know he was safe in New York. Before he could check his calendar, his cell phone was ringing. Not paying attention to the caller ID, Morgan assumed it was Kyna returning his call.

"Hey, baby. How are you doing without me?"

"Eww, Morgan. This is your sister," Melissa tried to sound grossed out.

"Melissa? I thought you were someone else," he said with a chuckle.

"That phone you have has caller ID. Please use it from now on."

"What is it that you want?"

"Mother has been looking for you. I told her you were on vacation for a week. She has been concerned; I think you need to talk to her."

Marilyn Hawkins was the true rock of the Hawkins family. She held everything together when things were going wrong. Whether they wanted to admit it or not, the Hawkins siblings needed their mother.

"I'll call her now. Do you know if she is in New York?" His parents maintained their family home in New York and had a condo in Florida, in the same building as Morgan.

"The parentals are in New York this week. You should just go over to the house. I'm on my way now; Mom cooked."

"Mom cooked, or she had dinner catered?" Morgan asked before getting too excited for a home-cooked meal.

"She said she cooked. You know what that means?"

"Sweet potato pie. I'm on my way."

Morgan ended the call with his sister and instructed his driver of their new destination. His driver had been with him since he made his first million dollars. Jesse Juarez, his driver and sometimes bodyguard, was a retired Navy Seal. He was quiet and observant. The man rarely said more than a few words.

Morgan sat in the back seat of the sedan and couldn't keep his mind from thinking about the week he just spent with his wife. His wife. Morgan couldn't get over the giddy feeling when he thought about Kyna. She was so beautiful and intelligent, and he couldn't believe she had agreed to marry him on a whim like that. They had an undeniable attraction, and everything just seemed right.

Having known Kyna for less than 48 hours, then getting married was crazy, and he was sure when their families found out, they would say the same thing, but he didn't care. Whenever he thought about her, his heart would swell and fill with a love he didn't know he had.

Morgan hadn't realized they were sitting in front of his parent's house on Long Island until he heard a tapping on his window. He gazed out and saw his sister staring at him with a bewildered look. Melissa stepped back when he opened the door and stepped out.

"What's that look for?" he asked.

"I was going to ask you the same thing. You looked lost in a good thought," Melissa smiled, then frowned. "Oh, were you thinking about that woman?"

"What woman?"

"The woman you thought I was when I called? Oh my God, you were thinking about her. She really put it on you. I have never seen you daydream and smiling like that before."

Morgan grabbed his sister in a loose headlock, "It's not what you think, and keep this to yourself."

"Mr. Hawkins, will you need anything else?" Jesse asked.

He released his sister to respond, "Jesse, I will probably be here for a while."

"You know you are welcomed to come inside and have dinner with us, Jesse," Melissa offered. She had dropped her voice an octave, trying to flirt with him. She had been doing that since he was hired.

"Thank you, Ms. Hawkins, but I am fine out here." Jesse nodded his head and returned to the driver's side of the vehicle.

Morgan followed Melissa to the back of their childhood home. He loved this house, and the first opportunity he had, he paid the mortgage off for his parents. Other than the loan his father gave him to start his business, the house was the only gift they allowed Morgan to give them. His mother claimed they didn't need to live an extravagant lifestyle, but she never returned any of the Mother's Day jewelry her children gave her either.

The family entrance to the house was in the rear, into the kitchen. The front door was only used for special occasions and non–family. Everyone who visited regularly knew to come into the house from the rear.

"There's my baby," Marilyn kissed Morgan on both cheeks before accepting his embrace. "Let me look at you. I haven't seen you in months."

"Mom, you saw me two weeks ago when John and I came over to watch the game with Dad."

"Well, it feels like months. Come on in. I have your favorite...macaroni and cheese," she said, already walking away toward the oven.

Morgan had an uneasy feeling. His mother was up to something and he wasn't sure what it was. He looked to

Melissa for some help, but she was too busy reading the ingredients label on a tub of yogurt in the refrigerator.

Ever since Melissa went on a health and fitness retreat last month, she has been into all-natural and organic foods. That thought reminded him of Kyna. She also paid close attention to the foods she consumed. Morgan remembered some of the foods they talked about. Kyna preferred fresh vegetables to can or frozen and would be a vegan if she didn't love cheese and chicken so much.

"There goes that goofy smile again. It looks good on you, big brother," Melissa smiled.

"Not one word," Morgan warned through clenched teeth.

The family sat down to have dinner when Morgan noticed a fifth place setting. He was sure John was still out of town, so the place setting couldn't be for him. Just when he was about to ask about it, the doorbell rang.

"Oh, I will get that," Marilyn smiled and flaunted over to the door.

"Dad, tell me she didn't invite some woman over here for me to *get to know*?" Morgan asked, using air quotes.

"Fine, I won't tell you." His father laughed and took his seat at the head of the table. "I learned a long time ago, whatever goes on in your mother's head is not for me to understand."

Morgan heard voices and mentally tried to come up with a reason to leave. He wasn't fast enough.

"Dahlia, you remember my husband and my children, Morgan and Melissa."

"Yes, I do. Hello everyone," Dahlia said. Morgan noticed she had a New England accent. Her voice wasn't as soft and alluring as Kyna's.

"Morgan, Dahlia is in town visiting her parents. You remember the Jackson's, don't you?" His mother asked with a wink of the eye.

"Yes, Mother. The Jackson's from Boston."

"Well, I invited Dahlia to dine with us because her parents are attending an art show this evening, and I didn't want her in that house all alone. Please, Dahlia, have a seat next to Morgan." Marilyn all but pushed the woman into the chair.

Morgan could kill his mother if he didn't love her so much. The dinner was pleasant enough. Dahlia was a nice girl, but she didn't have the fire that Kyna had. Dahlia was much more reserved and quiet, almost shy. At the end of dinner, Morgan didn't want to be rude, so he tried to excuse himself from the table, but his mother wasn't having it. She kept them all hostage by continuing to tell stories and engage them in conversations. Being rude was looking like his only chance to escape when his phone rang.

"Excuse me, Father, ladies, I must take this call," Morgan stood to his feet and exited the room.

"I thought you would never call me back."

"I'm sorry. I fell asleep and when I woke, it took me a minute to realize where I was. You weren't next to me and I thought I may have been dreaming, but I looked down at my hand and knew it was all real."

*****

Kyna had called her sisters and friends when she returned home. She desperately wanted to tell someone about her dream. She had met a gorgeous billionaire, talked to him all night and married him the next day. At least she thought it was a dream, until she looked at the five-carat wedding ring on her left hand. Reality quickly set in and she remembered every glorious detail.

She jumped to her feet and ran to her closet, but it looked the same. Where were her new clothes and accessories? Kyna went into her living room and found what she was looking for. Three suitcases and two garment bags full of clothes, shoes, and accessories. Morgan told her to get anything she wanted. She hadn't splurged in Vegas, but when he whisked her away without allowing her to pack, she needed to get additional items for a different climate.

Kyna unpacked her belongings and placed them in the closet of her spare bedroom. Many of the items were too expensive for her salary and her sisters would know it if they ever saw it. They frequently visited her closet for things to borrow. She would have to explain the designer labels, and Kyna wasn't ready to do that. After unpacking, she realized she hadn't heard from Morgan. Her phone indicated she had a few missed calls from her sisters, but it was the text message she was stuck on.

MADE IT SAFELY, BUT MISSING YOU

"Oh, baby, it was all real." Morgan lowered his voice to a deep baritone. The sound of his voice sent shivers up her spine.

"Morgan, why are you whispering?" Kyna asked while whispering herself.

"Because, I am at my parent's house for dinner, and my mom is trying to play matchmaker." Morgan turned around to make sure no one was around or listening to him.

"Excuse me? You mean to tell me you are having dinner with another woman?" Kyna raised her voice back to a normal level, but couldn't keep the bitter tinge away.

"My jealous wife again," Morgan laughed. "You have nothing to worry about. I want only you."

Morgan wondered what Kyna thought would happen while they were keeping their marriage a secret. He was a single billionaire, and women repeatedly threw themselves at him. Did she believe all of the women would suddenly stop for no reason?

"I must admit, this is going to be challenging. Especially knowing your mother is going to try and find you a wife at all cost. I miss you already. Until we see each other again, I will work on my jealousy," Kyna snickered.

"I will call you this evening when I get home. I want your voice to be the last thing I hear before I sleep at night."

"Your wish is my command." Kyna ended the call and rolled over in her bed. She smiled so brightly, then kicked her feet in the air like a schoolgirl whose crush called her for the first time.

Kyna decided to find some food, but quickly realized that she didn't have anything in her refrigerator to eat. She dressed quickly in a pair of jeans and a pullover sweatshirt and ventured out to her favorite eating establishment. KoKo's was a small café with the best fried chicken in the city. She entered to the heavenly smell of soul food at its best.

"Hey KoKo," Kyna announced when she saw the owner sitting behind her desk.

"Hey, my favorite nurse. Ya looking good. Ya glowing gurl, where've ya been?" KoKo asked in her heavy southern accent.

"I took a little vacation in Mexico." Kyna smiled, thinking of her amazing honeymoon.

"Well, that little vacation did wonders for ya. Ya were always beautiful, but now ya are... Wait, what's that on your finger?"

Kyna had forgotten to take her ring off and put it away. Precisely what she didn't want to happen was unwanted attention. She decided to play it off and pretend it wasn't a real diamond.

"Oh, this? I picked it up in a gift shop. Looks real, doesn't it?"

"It sure does." KoKo got a little closer to inspect the ring, but Kyna placed her hands in her pockets. KoKo backed away, "Ya want ya usual?"

"Yes please." She exhaled, glad to have dodged that bullet. If KoKo had gotten any closer, she would have known they were real diamonds.

Kyna always ordered the same meal - a six-wing special with an added side of macaroni and cheese and collard greens. KoKo made her mac and cheese the cheesiest, just the way Kyna and her sisters loved it. While she waited for her order to be completed, Kyna sat in a corner and recalled her last week and her husband. She was still finding it difficult to believe she was actually married.

In her wildest dreams, Kyna never envisioned herself being married. She knew she wanted to be a nurse and help people. Once she started working in nursing, she couldn't stop learning. So, she went back to school to get her bachelor's and master's degree in nursing, then another master's degree in healthcare management. Finally, she decided to get her doctorate in nursing.

Some people thought she was crazy for getting a doctorate degree in nursing when she could have gone to medical school, but after already having years in clinical nursing, she really wanted to work in research. That is where her passion was. When the hospital director found out about her academic accomplishments, he paired her with a new doctor to the hospital to study reproductive therapies in high-risk women.

Dr. Grant Hawkins was revered as an obstetrician. She was excited to work with him until she met his ego first. He was a handsome man, and Kyna could see how women went crazy for his charm and good looks. When they first met, he acted as if she were his personal assistant. Kyna was answering phones and taking messages from his admirers outside and within the hospital. She gritted her teeth and did as he asked until the hospital director made the formal introductions. Dr. Grant then humbled himself, and their working relationship had been manageable. Now, she thought it was crazy that she was married to his brother.

Kyna returned home to enjoy her meal and checked her cell phone, noticing a missed call from her sister Karmyn. If she didn't call her sister back, Karmyn would just show up on her doorstep, unannounced. Karmyn did not like to be ignored.

"Hey, sister. What's up?"

"Glad you made it back from the mountains safe and sound."

Kyna had forgotten she told her sisters she was taking an R&R vacation at a friend's cabin. She didn't think of how she would explain her tan to her sisters or her friends. Quickly, Kyna changed the story.

"Oh, I decided to go to the beach instead. I got an Airbnb in Miami," she babbled and had to stop herself from saying too much.

"Ok, well, I was calling to see if you wanted to go shopping next weekend?" Karmyn asked. They both enjoyed discount shopping.

Kyna knew that Morgan would be with her next weekend because she had gotten a copy of his schedule from Raven. This would be the tricky part, trying to navigate between her secret married life and her sisters. How would she be able to balance the two without them being suspicious?

"My director put me on a new project. Let me see how involved it will be, and I will let you know." Kyna didn't exactly lie; she was working on a new project.

"Are you feeling okay?" Karmyn was the more perceptive sister. She could probably hear the nervousness in Kyna's voice.

"I'm good—just a little tired. You know how you need a vacation after the vacation. Well, I have some clothes to wash, and I have to prepare for work tomorrow. I'll call you later," Kyna rushed her sister off the phone.

"Okay, sister, talk to you then."

If her sister asked any more questions, Kyna wasn't sure she would be able to keep up the deceit. She finished her meal in peace and turned on the television while waiting for Morgan to call back. She was starting to drift asleep when Morgan finally called her for the night.

"I was beginning to wonder when you were going to call," she yawned. "I was falling asleep."

"I'm sorry, it's so late. I promise to do better."

"How was your date?" she asked, this time sounding nonchalant.

"She wasn't you." Morgan waited for a second to let that sink in before speaking again. "Do me a favor, open your bible."

"My bible?"

"Yes, you said you read your bible every night. Well, I want to read with you. I'm also going to find us a married couple's devotional to share with each other every night."

"I would like that." Kyna didn't think she could love this man any more than she did. Saying you are a God-fearing man and proving it were two different things. She had men tell her they believed in God, but only said it to see how far they could get with her. In college, a minister at her church tried to get her to sleep with him. When she told him she was waiting for marriage, he responded by ignoring her every Sunday.

Their first nightly bible study was the book of Esther. Kyna always loved reading about Queen Esther. They took turns reading a chapter, then discussed what each chapter was saying and why it was important.

"I can see why you love reading about Queen Esther," Morgan told her.

"Why is that?"

"You are so much like her. You are both beautiful and instantly caught the eye of your king. She was obedient without compromising her morals or ethics. She was fiercely loyal to her family and her people. She was fearless and stood up for what was the right thing to do, despite the consequences. You are my Queen Esther."

Chapter 6

Over the past six weeks, Morgan and Kyna had seen each other every weekend. Either they would hide out in her apartment or she would fly to wherever he was while he worked. They spent quality time together, continuing to get to know one another and creating new experiences. Kyna introduced him to new cuisines. She couldn't believe that Morgan had never tried Thai food. Drunken noodles were one of her favorites and something she shared with her sister, Kaleigh.

The weekend of the Stay Sharp Gala was approaching. Stay Sharp was a not-for-profit organization that provided entrepreneurial mentoring to teenagers. Her sister Karleigh and soon-to-be brother-in-law, Simon Sharp, created a co-working shared space where youth as young as 13 could benefit from courses, one-on-one business coaching, and networking with other entrepreneurs in the community. The gala was the annual fundraiser for the organization.

Kyna had selected several dresses for the evening and couldn't choose which one to wear. Instead, she decided she would have several wardrobe changes throughout the evening. She had spent all day in the research lab and couldn't wait to get home and soak in her bathtub before getting ready for the gala.

Driving through her community, Kyna hadn't seen anything out of the ordinary in her neighborhood, but something didn't feel right. She felt like someone was watching her. Instead of dwelling on the eerie feeling, she shook her head to clear her mind and walked into her house.

First, she smelled food cooking, then she heard music. That could only mean that Morgan was home. It was funny how no matter where they were, she always considered it home when they were together.

"Honey, I'm home," Kyna announced and laughed. In the kitchen, she found Morgan finalizing the smothered chicken, which was his specialty and her favorite of the dinners he had prepared for her. They chose to stay in more than go out to limit their exposure to the media.

"Right on time, my queen." He had started calling her that after they studied the book of Esther their first night away from one another.

"Oh, honey, everything looks delicious, but I thought I told you I was going to the gala tonight." She gave him a chaste kiss to the cheek, then used her finger to swipe a taste of the sauce.

"Is that why there are several gowns laid across your bed with matching shoes and accessories. I came in to take a nap and had to sleep on the sofa." He kissed her forehead, then her cheek and like every other time, he couldn't stop kissing her. Kyna loved that he enjoyed kissing her. But, that was also how things got heated between them.

"Stop, I don't have time for that. I need to soak in the tub and then get my hair and makeup ready." Kyna retreated from the kitchen and headed toward her bedroom.

"Which dress are you planning to wear?" Morgan asked, following behind her.

"All of them," she said before disappearing into the bedroom and closing the door behind her. After being married for seven weeks, she was still as giddy as their wedding night. She quickly undressed, tossing her scrubs into the laundry basket and heading into the bathroom. Kyna was surprised to find the bathtub was filled, and the water was still hot. She turned to call for Morgan, but he was standing in the doorway, holding a glass of wine.

"I want you to eat *good* food before heading to the gala and getting served that rubber chicken with the cold vegetables." Morgan handed her the glass of wine, "after your bath, your dinner will be served, and I promise to stay out of your way while you get ready."

"How did I get so lucky?" she asked, accepting the glass.

"Not lucky, but loved. Enjoy your bath." He winked and gave her a devious smile before closing the door behind him.

*****

Morgan watched Kyna as she took her time pampering herself. She had a system of how she bathed, moisturized her skin, styled her hair, and even applied her makeup. The whole process was intriguing to watch. She went through all of that preparation to look even more beautiful. And this was for a gala and not for him. That last thought made him begin to feel the jealous tingles.

He couldn't escort her to the gala. Attending would be risky, considering how his brothers were able to read him so well. Morgan was sure he wouldn't be able to keep his eyes from Kyna. So, he told his brothers to go as representatives of the Hawkins Group. Now, knowing what Kyna planned to wear and seeing her made up, Morgan was thinking of ways to keep her home. This event was very important to Kyna and her sisters, so there was no way he could stop her from attending. The sisters loved and supported each other fiercely.

She finished her preparations, short of her lip color, and sat down to eat her dinner before getting fully dressed. She sat across from Morgan, wearing only her silk robe. The temptation was eating away at him.

"Why are you staring at me?" Kyna asked between bites of food.

"Because you are so beautiful. And I am wondering how I got this lucky."

She returned his words back to him, "You're not lucky, you're loved."

Morgan continued to watch her eat and began wondering how she would handle things when the world found out that he was officially off the market. For years, the media had portrayed him as the number one bachelor. Women of all ages made attempts for him, and all were unsuccessful. Before meeting Kyna, he had not been romantically involved with a woman in almost a year. His focus had been on building his company. Now, his new focus was on building a legacy for his family with Kyna.

*****

Kyna had only finished half of her meal before she jumped up to get dressed. Morgan often fed her too much food, and she needed to work out twice a day to maintain her figure. She went into her bedroom to get dressed in just enough time before Karmyn arrived to pick her up for the evening.

On the two occasions when a sister stopped by unannounced, Morgan had to hide out in Kyna's spare bedroom. The sisters liked to share their clothing, drink wine and talk. The last time Karleigh stopped by, Morgan thought Kyna forgot he was there. The sisters talked and drank through two bottles of wine. Eventually, Morgan had to send a text message to Kyna and remind her he was waiting.

Kyna stepped out of her room wearing a rose gold mini-skirt dress. The back had a cape tail that dragged the floor even in Kyna's four-inch heels. The bodice dipped low and was covered in jewels of varying colors.

"Baby, you look stunning. I think you would look even better with this." Morgan pulled a diamond necklace with matching diamond earrings from a box he was hiding under the table.

"Oh my God, is this the Buccellati Fiamma set?"

"The one and only," Morgan replied. He stepped behind her and placed the necklace that had 1600 diamonds around her neck. "I was hoping you didn't think it would be too gaudy."

"It's beautiful," were the only words she could manage to say.

"The design made me think of flames, and that made me think of my super hot wife," he grabbed her around the waist and kissed her neck.

"Morgan, I love it, but I can't wear this. It's too expensive." Kyna attempted to take the necklace off, but Morgan stopped her, taking her hands in his.

"You can wear it, and if anyone asks, tell them it's cubic zirconia or one of those direct sales jewelry companies you love so much."

Kyna laughed. "It may work, because there is no way I could afford this."

"I also think you need security. You will draw too much attention of the male persuasion in this dress."

"You are so funny. I'll be fine," she tried to reassure him. "I'll be with my sisters. Plus, Nick and Simon will be there and, of course, the other Hawkins brothers."

"I've seen your sisters; they are just as beautiful as you. I think you all need security. Let me send Jesse with you."

"Absolutely not. I would have to explain who he is and his presence. No. Trust me, I will be fine." Kyna reassured Morgan once again that she would be okay. She loved how he cared for her and wanted to keep her safe. She knew that there would be a need for security in the near future, but she wanted to feel like a regular person right now. Kyna wasn't sure she could feel normal with $675,000 worth of diamonds around her neck.

"It's not you I don't trust; it's the men at the gala." He rubbed his head and exhaled with a low whistle. "Be extra careful. I love you." He was about to lean in to kiss her cheek so not to ruin her lipstick when the doorbell rang.

"Kyna, let's go. You better be ready," Karmyn yelled from the door.

"My sister knows me well." Kyna grabbed her garment bag and sparkle handbag and walked to the door. She whispered, "Love you much. See you soon."

Morgan did trust her, but seeing her dressed up and looking beautiful, he just didn't trust other people, specifically men. He peered through the front window's blinds and watched Karmyn pull out of the driveway and down the street, then called Jesse. He was usually discreet and Morgan was confident he could handle this little task.

"Jesse, I need you to head to the JW and keep an eye on Kyna and her sisters."

"Anything in particular I need to look for?" Jesse asked.

"No. And keep your distance. Kyna will be mad if she sees you."

"No problem, Mr. Hawkins."

Knowing that Jesse would be there from a distance gave Morgan a little peace. For the rest of the evening, Morgan worked on a new acquisition deal that he hoped would be lucrative. Melissa had brought this company to his attention, and after reviewing their portfolio, he agreed with her initial assessment. The current owner may not like the corporate takeover that was about to occur, but it was a sound investment. The company just needed the right marketing team to take them to the next level.

Morgan was sitting at the small desk in Kyna's bedroom, nodding off while working on his laptop. He was trying to stay awake until Kyna came home. The clicking of the locks on the front door jarred him awake. The blaring red numbers of the bedside clock indicated that it was four o'clock in the morning. That couldn't be right; his wife had not stayed out until 4 A.M. Morgan reached across the desk for his cell phone and saw three messages from Jesse and none from Kyna. Jesse's first message said everything was ok; the second message said Kaleigh was going home with Nick, a family friend. The third message from Jesse stated that Kyna and Karmyn met two guys at Denny's. That was an hour ago.

Kyna eased the door open and jumped when she saw Morgan sitting at the desk in the bedroom.

"Morgan! I didn't think you would be awake," she nervously shuffled her garment bag and shoes from one hand to the other.

"Well, I am. How was your evening?" Morgan tried to sound indifferent in his questioning. Instead, he sounded accusatorial.

"The gala was fabulous. Thanks to Karleigh having her own suite in the hotel, I was able to make three wardrobe changes without any issues." Kyna quickly breezed past Morgan and placed her items in the closet.

"I'm sure you were beautiful in each dress." Morgan stood to his full height and stretched, giving a big yawn for good measure.

"Are you okay?" Kyna stood in front of him and wrapped her arms around his waist. Morgan tried to gently remove her arms, but he may have gripped too tightly.

"Kyna, I'm tired. Let's just go to bed." He walked to the other side of the bed, away from her and slipped out of his pants.

"Morgan! Something is wrong. Please talk to me."

"Nothing is wrong. I fell asleep working and now I just want to go to bed. Good night, *Wife*." He spat the word "wife" from his lips and didn't give her another glance.

The next morning Morgan awoke to an empty bed. He was prepared for Kyna to be upset and have an attitude because he went to sleep with his own attitude. The proper action to take would have been to talk about how he felt, but he let his anger get in the way. Wives were not supposed to be out in the street without their husbands that late at night, and they certainly shouldn't be out with other men.

He sat up in the bed, planning to take a shower and then find his wife so they could talk. He didn't have to search because she walked into the room carrying a tray of breakfast food.

"What is all of this?" he asked.

"I figured that you were upset about the time I came in last night. I should have texted you, but I was having so much fun with my sister and our cousins from Philadelphia that I forgot to let you know I would be out late." She placed the tray on the bed between the two of them.

Morgan felt like a fool. She was with her cousins. Of course, her family was in attendance; the gala was a big night for Karleigh and her fiancé. He was about to apologize for getting upset, but Kyna placed a strip of bacon to his lips, preventing him from speaking.

"Husband, I will never do that again. I promise, if I am going to stay out late, I will text or call you first." She kissed him gently on the lips, then fed him the bacon.

This was why he loved her so much; she was understanding and loving. Even when she had a right to be upset with him, she wasn't. They continued to feed each other breakfast until their plates loaded with bacon, sausage, eggs, and pancakes were wiped dry.

After breakfast, they showered and dressed, preparing to spend the day together, just lounging around the house. They had limited places they could go without risking being seen by someone they knew. Kyna wasn't ready for her sisters to be in her business, especially with Poe's work relationship with Morgan and her work relationship with Grant. Kyna told him there would be too many questions. Morgan didn't want his brothers to know for similar reasons. Their marriage and relationship was still new, and after last night, it was also fragile.

The two of them watched old movies and ordered food from a local taco bar. The sun was beginning to set when Morgan felt that he had to tell her about Jesse following her all night. Keeping secrets and lying by omission was not how he wanted his marriage to be.

"Queen, we need to talk."

Chapter 7

Kyna felt uncomfortable when Morgan said those words. Usually, the woman would say those words when she was about to break her lover's heart. Her face must have expressed her angst because Morgan held her hands in his and used his thumb to soothe her erratic emotions.

"It's not whatever you are thinking," he calmly said.

"Are you sure?"

"I'm sure. Although, once you hear what I have to say, you may still get angry with me."

"You mean, once you say something like, I had Jesse follow you last night." She raised an eyebrow challenging him to deny it.

Morgan dropped her hands and his jaw at the same time. Served him right to think she wouldn't noticed Jesse lurking in the corners of the ballroom or him parking across the street from the Denny's.

"H..H..How did you know?" Shocked, Morgan stumbled over his words.

"He is not as covert as he thinks and should work on that. I first spotted him when I was dancing with Simon on the dancefloor. At first, I thought he was attending with John and Grant, but when I saw him parked across the street from the Denny's and the parking lot was almost empty, his Lincoln stood out like a sore thumb."

Morgan laughed. "Are you upset with me?"

"I was, but I understood that you just wanted me safe. And I must say, I was looking extraordinarily sexy last night. How could I be mad that you are looking after my safety? But, I will say that I was annoyed at first."

"Annoyed, I can deal with, but I never want to upset you." Morgan kissed her hands, first her knuckles, then her palms. Then he traced soft kisses up her arms until he reached her neck. Kyna let a giggle escape before he reached her lips. That sealed the deal.

Kyna awakened early Sunday morning to make breakfast again for her husband before she had to leave for church. This became their routine. She would kiss him goodbye and leave for church, and he would return to work, wherever that was in the world. At times Kyna felt sad because she had recently begun feeling like keeping their marriage a secret wasn't being truthful or honest to their families. She also wondered what her sisters would think when they found out.

She reached over in the bed and found Morgan gone, and the sheets were cold. That meant he had been out of bed for some time. Kyna slipped into her robe and pulled the belt tight around her waist before she went in search of her husband. Her apartment was small, so she didn't have to go far to find Morgan in the spare bedroom with his head over his laptop and quietly speaking into his phone.

"Don't worry about that, I can be there. It doesn't matter. I will make it work. For you, anything," he said with a dry laugh.

Those phrases were the same words he had said to her when they were apart. Kyna couldn't help but feel gullible at the moment. She started questioning herself. Was Morgan too good to be true? Did they move too fast? Her mind was running a mile a minute.

Kyna attempted to move away from the door when Morgan jerked his head up and stared intensely into her eyes. Without breaking their connection, he ended his call and turned in his chair to fully face her.

"My queen, I didn't know you were awake."

"I was going to start breakfast," Kyna nervously bit her bottom lip. "I didn't mean to disturb you."

"Nonsense. You are a beautiful distraction, but a distraction I love."

"Okay, well, let me go get started." She hastily turned away so he wouldn't see the tears of doubt forming in her eyes.

"Not so fast. Come back, please."

Kyna found it near impossible to resist his deep, sultry voice. She slowly turned around and couldn't stop the tears that fell.

Morgan motioned for her to come closer. Then he patted his lap, indicating he wanted her to sit there. "What is all of this about?"

Kyna complied. He took the pads of his thumbs and wiped the tears away. She was becoming a jealous, emotional mess. "I don't know. I think maybe it's time we let our secret out of the bag."

She watched his expression change and was unable to detect what he was thinking. "If that's really what you want. But I have a feeling that's not why you are crying."

"Morgan, who were you talking to on the phone just now?" Kyna decided to be open with him.

He held her and tightened his grip around her waist, "That was the marketing director of the hotel we purchased in Dubai."

"It's seven o'clock in the morning on a Sunday," she stated with doubt.

"But, it is three in the afternoon in Dubai. I wanted to go over some information with them before you woke."

Kyna looked away, utterly embarrassed for jumping the gun with jealousy. She was so sure that he was talking to someone else. Being the great guy that Morgan is, he didn't mention her jealousy; he just changed the subject altogether.

Morgan kissed her cheek and asked, "Hey, how did you sleep?"

"Thanks to you, very well." That made her smile because her night with her husband was amazing. Kyna stood, "I was about to start breakfast. Will you join me?" She knew he was going to say yes, but thought it was a nice gesture to ask.

"As long as you are making waffles," he raised his eyebrows up and down. "Let me finish up some work things and I will be right in."

Kyna headed to the kitchen with the intent to make the best waffles her husband had ever had. She was grateful that Morgan didn't hold her temporary jealous incidents against her. That was one of the many characteristics about him that she loved. He didn't keep a record of anything only to throw it up in your face later, especially where she was concerned. When Kyna had a bout of jealousy or had disagreements, it was like water under the bridge the next day.

Morgan pitched in to help with the breakfast buffet that Kyna was preparing. The mix was ready for the waffles and the bacon was on the stove-top grill. She watched him take the veggies from the refrigerator and begin to cut and chop. A man who was good in the kitchen was a major turn-on. Kyna smiled as her husband sauteed the spinach and mushrooms for the veggie omelets.

In no time at all, they were seated at the kitchen table. Morgan held Kyna's hand and blessed the food before they began to devour it. They didn't talk during their meal; enjoying the food's taste was something they both enjoyed savoring, uninterrupted. After breakfast, Morgan began clearing away the dishes from the table.

"What are your plans for next weekend?" Morgan asked while placing the dishes in the dishwasher.

"I may be free; I will know better after Wednesday. What's up?" she responded while wiping the table clean. They worked well together and didn't feel like either was in the other's way.

"I want to spend some time in the mountains."

"Is everything okay?" Kyna was a little concerned that he would take time away from his business so soon after their honeymoon to vacation in the mountains. Before they married, he admitted he never vacationed.

"Yes, everything is okay. But, I remember you saying you liked going to Gatlinburg to relax. I thought it may be a good idea to spend our three-month anniversary there.

Kyna was overwhelmed by his thoughtfulness. He was planning anniversary trips, and she loved it.

"Do you want me to call my friend and see if his cabin is available?"

Morgan laughed, "No, I purchased a cabin for us. Actually, I purchased several cabins for you."

She scrunched her face creating the lines of confusion between her brows, she asked, "For me? Just for me?"

"Yes. Just for you." Morgan placed the last plate in the dishwasher. Drying his hands on a dishtowel, he continued, "Another stream of income for you. Cabins in the Gatlinburg area are very profitable. After breakfast, I can go over all the details with you. Basically, you own 12 cabins, and Mountain Top Property Management will be overseeing the rentals. You will get a monthly payment that you can use, however you want."

Kyna relaxed her face, then cocked it to the side, peering at her husband. She wondered when Morgan would stop with the expensive gifts. She didn't want his money or need his gifts to prove he loved her. "When were you going to tell me about the properties?"

"I was planning to tell you today. It's an anniversary gift," he winked at her.

"Morgan, I know you are filthy rich..."

"We are filthy rich, baby," he corrected her, then started the dishwasher.

Kyna had to speak loudly over the sound of the dishwasher. She was sure he did that on purpose. "You don't need to spend so much money on me. I am a simple woman."

"The clothes in your closet say otherwise," he laughed.

He was right. Kyna liked to shop and she loved clothes, but she was frugal. Her shopping addiction was fueled by getting a good deal. She never met a clearance sale that didn't have her name on it. "Seriously, your gifts are too lavish. It's too much and not necessary."

Kyna watched him approach her with a sad face. She laughed because he was attempting to pout. "I enjoy making you happy and my job is to keep that smile on your face," he said with a soft kiss.

She kissed him back as a way of saying thank you. Kyna couldn't stay mad at him for long. He was always thinking of her and providing for her. She couldn't ask for anything more. But, in the back of her mind, she wondered if she would be enough for him. He had everything he wanted. With a phone call, he had stores opening at midnight just for him to shop. Kyna couldn't help but think he would tire of her at some point.

While they were kissing, Kyna heard her phone ring in the distance.

"Please don't answer that," Morgan murmured against her lips.

"I have to. It's Karmyn's ringtone."

Kyna raced to find her phone before the ringing stopped. She found the phone in her handbag that she had thrown on the sofa when she came home early that morning.

"Hey, sister. What's wrong?"

"It's Poe. Get over to her house right now. She won't let me take her to the hospital," she sounded frantic.

"Okay, let me get dressed and I will be right there." Kyna tossed her phone and raced into the bedroom. Whatever was wrong with Poe, it was bad enough that Karmyn had to call her.

"Everything okay?" Morgan asked, following Kyna into the bedroom.

"No, Poe is not well. Karmyn is at her place now. I need to get dressed and get over there." Kyna grabbed the first dress appropriate for church from her closet and tossed it on the bed. She then headed to her bathroom. A quick shower was all she had time for. Kyna sleeked her hair into a ponytail and put on some lip gloss. She was able to accomplish all of this in 30 minutes.

*****

Morgan watched her spin around the room like a tornado. He had never seen her get dressed and ready to go anywhere that fast. He mentally noted that she could get ready quickly if she wanted to. She grabbed her purse and jacket, pasted a chaste kiss to Morgan's lips and was out the door tossing a quick "*I love you*" over her shoulder as she closed the door behind her.

Usually, after Kyna left for church, Morgan would watch the live streaming church service of Kyna's church. On her way home from their family dinner, she would call him and discuss the pastor's sermon. That was just another way they tried to stay connected to God and one another. After three months, they still read the bible together most nights before going to bed.

Chapter 8

Morgan had intended to celebrate three months of marriage in the mountains with his wife. But business meeting after meeting, that couldn't get rescheduled, prevented them from going. It didn't help that Kyna was also very busy in her lab and with her research.

As a consolation prize, he sent Kyna a diamond bangle bracelet and three dozen roses to celebrate their anniversary since he couldn't get away. Their trip to the mountains didn't happen until the following month. At least they would be able to celebrate four months together.

The mountain air and seclusion was just the solution they both needed to decompress from their demanding careers. Morgan arrived at the cabin before his wife and was able to prepare a romantic dinner. He was putting the finishing touches on the Waldorf salad when Kyna walked through the door. She was just as breathtaking as she was the first time he saw her.

"Morgan?" Kyna called out, dropping her bag on the floor by the door. "Something smells good."

"Hello, my queen," he greeted her with a soul-stirring kiss.

Morgan watched as Kyna looked around the cabin with amazement. She stopped in the center of the great room and turned in circles.

"This is not a cabin; this is a chalet," she said with astonishment.

"Go big or go home, right?" Morgan responded, smiling.

Kyna continued to walk around the cabin's first floor, opening doors and checking out the rooms. "How many bedrooms does it have?" she yelled from somewhere. Morgan had returned to the kitchen to finish preparing dinner.

"I considered the number of rooms before buying this particular cabin. There are 10 bedrooms, all with their own attached bathrooms and wood-burning fireplaces. Four bedrooms on the second level have an additional sitting room attached. I wanted to keep with the area's cabin-like theme, so the dining room has 4 picnic benches instead of a formal dining table. Our families can vacation together here," he answered from the kitchen.

Kyna reappeared from behind the staircase that led from the second floor into the kitchen. "You're doing it again. This is too much. Why do you spend so much of your money?" she asked, taking a seat at the breakfast bar.

"Because I can't take it with me when I die," Morgan joked.

"I'm serious, Morgan. You spend money like it's water. I admit I have a shopping fetish, and I enjoy eating out, but I'm also cost-conscious. I usually make my purchases with reward points, or the items are on sale. You, just drop a million dollars like it's nothing," she pouted.

Morgan loved that she wasn't married to him for his money. She rarely used her credit card since he paid it off. But, she had to learn to accept their wealth. "Kyna..." Morgan spread his hands across the breakfast bar and stared intently into her eyes. "I told you before, I like to make you happy."

"But receiving gifts is not my love language," she returned his serious gaze.

Together, they had read the book *Love Languages* and discussed the results of their assessment. Morgan didn't like the book and thought it oversimplified the intricacies of relationships and love. Kyna felt the opposite and often referred to statements from the text, especially regarding her love language.

"I know what your love language is, and mine is giving. I enjoy giving to my queen. Indulge me, please," he smiled and returned to cooking. "Besides, you love your family like I love mine. This is just another investment that everyone can benefit from.

"Okay. After we eat, can I get the official tour of this place?"

They enjoyed a meal of grilled lemon dill salmon and baked potatoes before going on the tour. Only one bedroom, their bedroom, had furniture. Morgan wanted Kyna to put her touch on the cabin in every room. This was her house, and he wanted to make sure she knew it. Of course, she could use any decorator she wanted, but he had a feeling she would do the decorating herself.

They stood in front of the massive window in their bedroom that overlooked the Great Smokey Mountains. Kyna held a cup of hot chocolate in her hands and leaned into Morgan's embrace. "Why did you buy such a huge chalet?" Kyna whispered.

"I want to begin a tradition where we can get our families together a few times a year. Once we announce to the world that we are married, our families will have minimal opportunities for privacy while gathering together. Did you notice that there is only one way up this mountain and the entrance is gated and guarded?" he asked.

Morgan selected the property for its security and privacy. The cabin was located high in the Great Smokey Mountains, overlooking Gatlinburg. There was enough parking for up to 20 vehicles, and just through the trees was a landing area for a helicopter. The cabin used to belong to a British entertainer, someone Morgan had never heard of.

He was grateful that Kyna had not brought up the cost of the cabin or decorating expenses. She would have to learn to accept that she was now the wife of a billionaire. Plus, she may faint at the price tag. Morgan was serious when he told her it was an investment.

The next day, Morgan and Kyna ventured out into public together. They both wore jeans, large pullover sweatshirts, baseball caps, and sunglasses to disguise themselves as much as possible. No one would recognize Kyna, but Morgan was often the subject of the paparazzi's affection. They had to keep a low profile, but that was nearly impossible when Kyna mentioned the amount of fun to be had on the Pigeon Forge side of the mountain.

They spent the day on the strip riding go-karts, playing putt-putt golf, horseback riding and ziplining. Morgan had to admit he had not had that much fun in years.

Sunday, they slept late, not wanting to leave the comforts of their bed. After brunch, they decided to go to Dollywood, an amusement park in Pigeon Forge built by the great country singer, Dolly Parton. Morgan encouraged Kyna to ride every single roller coaster and have as much ice cream as she could handle. She had just stepped inside the gift store when Morgan heard his name being called from behind him.

"Morgan! Is that you, Morgan?"

Before the woman could get too close, Jesse, who had been the couple's shadow every time they went out, blocked her path.

"Morgan, honey, it's me, Bridget," she waved her hand incessantly.

Morgan motioned to Jesse to let her through. If he didn't, he would never hear the end of it. Bridget Vandersloot was the daughter of one of his business associates. She had been trying to attach herself to him for years. Bridget was an attractive woman and very successful in the fashion industry, but she was an elitist and opportunist.

"Funny seeing you here," she said just before throwing her arms around his neck. Kyna chose that exact moment to exit the store.

Morgan grabbed Bridget's arms and extricated himself from her grasp as Kyna approached. "Kyna, I would like for you to meet Bridget Vandersloot. Bridget, this is my friend, Kyna." He didn't want to give Bridget too much information. Along with being an opportunist, she was also a gossip of the worst kind.

Bridget barely gave Kyna a glance. But, the look Kyna gave her spoke volumes.

"Are you attending the concert tonight? I'm here with Jackson Wilmington. He's headlining tonight," Bridget said in her cheery voice. Morgan was accustomed to Bridget, always name-dropping the celebrities and entertainers she knew.

Instead of answering Bridget's question, he placed his arm around Kyna's waist and said, "We were just leaving."

"Well, we haven't seen you at the vineyard this year. I was hoping to talk to you," she glanced at Kyna before continuing. "Privately... about a new business venture."

Morgan pulled Kyna closer, flush against his side, hoping to let Bridget know he had other plans.

"I doubt I will be making it to the vineyard this year. I have other priorities to attend to."

"Well, I hope those *priorities* don't keep you away long."

"They will," Kyna answered and kept her smile intact, although her smile didn't reach her eyes.

Bridget tossed her hair back before saying, "Morgan, I see that you've downgraded the women you date now. I have friends of a higher caliber."

"That's enough, Bridget," Morgan dropped his voice to a lethal whisper, causing Bridget to take a step backward.

Morgan felt Kyna's hand rest just above his heart. She used her sweet, gentle voice to calm him down. "Morgan, don't. Let's just leave." He turned to his wife and saw compassion and love in her eyes. Instead of addressing Bridget again and giving her any more attention, they turned and walked away.

After the couple left Bridget standing alone, slack-jawed, they stood outside the front gates in silence. Neither knowing what to say while they waited for Jesse to bring the car around.

Morgan felt he had to apologize for the scene that just occurred. That was unlike him, allowing someone the ability to cause his rage. Bridget came close to feeling all of his wrath. He wouldn't allow anyone to disrespect his wife, even if they didn't know who she was.

"Baby, I'm sorry about her condescension. I have more than my fair share of elitist friends." He was rubbing his hands up and down her arms, more for his benefit than hers.

"Morgan, she didn't bother me. But, I have never heard you speak in anger to anyone before. Not like that. That kinda scared me."

The thought that he scared her hadn't crossed his mind. Kyna was right; she had never seen his ruthless side. He usually reserved that tone for business matters. Rarely has he had to be so direct with someone in a public or personal setting. Morgan gazed into her eyes; he never wanted her to fear him for any reason.

"There are times when I get angry, but I never want you to be afraid of me. I would never hurt you." They communicated through their eyes. He waited until her body relaxed under his fingertips, and she gave him a smile that was full of innuendo.

Jesse pulled the car up to the curb just in front of them. Morgan helped her inside of the sedan and gently closed the door. He let out a long, slow breath before walking around the car and entering from the other side. Morgan dodged a bullet with this one; he just hoped that was the last one.

During the drive back to the cabin, Kyna remained quiet and that panicked Morgan. She wasn't her usual bubbly self. He silently prayed that she did not have any doubts. They had discussed that there would be women who would openly throw themselves at him. He was an attractive billionaire and that attracted women of all ages.

Once at the cabin, Kyna didn't stop. Instead, she headed straight for the bedroom. Morgan was going crazy thinking about what was going on in her head. He needed answers and followed right behind her.

"Kyna. Talk to me, please," Morgan gently pleaded.

"What do you want me to say? I'm not afraid of you and I am not upset. I'm just shocked. That woman was more than rude and condescending; she was just mean. I've had my run-ins with the type. You sounded like you were going to murder her. I know you won't hurt me. I'm pretty sure you wouldn't hurt her. But, what if that were a man? Would your anger cause you to hurt someone else?"

Morgan regarded her words very carefully. She knew him to get briefly jealous when it came to her, yet, her fear was for someone else. He didn't know what to make of her feelings or his. How could he get her to understand? He felt it was his responsibility as her husband to protect her. Even from villainous and spiteful women they may come across. Morgan was sure there would be more attacks once their marriage became public.

Morgan hesitantly walked closer to Kyna. "Queen, I can't promise that I will contain my anger toward someone if that person attacks you in any way. But I will promise that if faced with a situation that flares my anger, I will think of you first, before I react."

Kyna seemed to think over his words first before responding, "I guess that is all I can ask for." She gave him that wicked smile and Morgan knew that meant all was well with them for now. He would accept their truce if it kept a smile on her face.

*****

Kyna arrived to work wearing the biggest smile. Her memories from the weekend carried over all week and she couldn't stop thinking about her husband. She knew she would have to let the cat out of the bag eventually, but she was happy they decided to remain private for a while.

She opened her office door to find Dr. Hawkins leaning against her desk, patiently waiting for her. The family resemblance was striking. Morgan and Grant had the same whiskey-colored eyes and strong jawline. Morgan's lips were fuller than Grant's. She was startled from her reverie when Grant spoke.

"Nurse Kyna," he nodded, taking a sip from his coffee cup while handing her a cup with his other hand.

"No. Whatever it is, you will have to figure that thing out with my sister all on your own." She grabbed the hot cup of coffee Grant was holding. He was trying to get on her good side in hopes she would help him get a date with Kaleigh.

"How do you know I need help with Kaleigh?" he asked.

"Because, I know my sister," Kyna stepped around Grant. She placed her bag on the floor beside her desk, then reached inside to grab her tennis shoes.

"Can you at least tell me how she is feeling?" Grant showed signs of genuine concern for her sister. He had been present for one of her health episodes.

"She has been better, but I think having no answers and no real diagnosis is what is bothering her the most." Kaleigh had been ill for some time. The doctors and specialists were unable to give her a diagnosis. Her sister's level of patience was far better than her own.

"Well, I want you to know that I care about your sister, and I want to be there for her."

This was the first time she had seen Grant drop his arrogant persona and truly look sincere. He had a pretentious way about him that Kyna despised. Since he met her sister, he started to appear like a regular guy in her eyes. "You will have to convince her yourself." Kyna smiled and sat at her desk as she watched the handsome doctor leave her office.

Kyna left work still in a great mood. On the way home, she stopped by the market and picked up some fresh salmon for dinner and a chocolate cake. She was feeling pretty good and thought she deserved a treat. She turned into her apartment complex and had that eerie feeling of being watched again. She looked all around and didn't see anything out of the norm. This was the third time in the past few months she had this feeling. She never considered herself paranoid, but this was becoming ridiculous. If it happened again, she was moving into the new and unused condo that Morgan bought for them.

Her phone began ringing as she was juggling her keys, groceries and work bag.

"Hello?" No answer. "Hello?"

Not having the time to play games, Kyna disconnected the call and tossed the phone into her bag. She walked into her apartment, disarmed the alarm system and noticed something out of place. Her kitchen window was slightly opened, and a dining room chair was pulled away from the table. Kyna always pushed her chairs up to the table and never opened her windows.

"Morgan! Are you here?" She didn't get an answer the first time, so she yelled out again. No response. Kyna began walking back toward the front door. She screamed when she bumped into something rock-solid that should not have been there. She turned to see Morgan holding two paper bags.

"You scared me half to death. Morgan, when did you get here?" Kyna placed her hand over her rapidly beating heart, attempting to catch her breath.

"I'm sorry, Queen. I've been here for about two hours. I came here first and started dinner. I got distracted by an email, then smelled the chicken burning. I opened the window to air the smoke from the room. Since I ruined dinner..." he held up the bag of Chinese food. "I went for take-out."

Kyna laughed at herself and the situation. That strange feeling she was having was really messing with her mind. She had a stellar security system in place, and it had been activated when she entered. She didn't need to be afraid of anything, but that didn't make the uneasiness she felt lessen any.

After dinner, Morgan wanted to watch a movie, but Kyna had other plans. She had missed her husband, and she intended to seduce him. They moved their party to the bedroom, where they stayed until Kyna awakened in the middle of the night.

She instinctively reached for her husband and only found cold sheets. She wondered how long he had been out of bed. Finding him missing in the middle of the night was becoming increasingly frustrating for her. Morgan worked hard, often spending the time they shared working on his laptop or taking calls from business associates. Kyna sometimes wondered if there was a place in his life for her. Sure he tried to make it all work, but he was beginning to spend more time with work than her. She understood his drive and determination to succeed. It was one reason she was attracted to him.

Wanting Morgan to wake her when he returned, she positioned herself in the bed to cover both sides. After a few minutes, which seemed like hours, Kyna got out of bed and made her way to the kitchen for a nighttime snack. She stopped when she heard Morgan on the phone. He was talking softly to the other person, and Kyna inwardly cringed because she hadn't heard him speak that way to her in some time. She didn't think the honeymoon phase was over yet, especially not after the night they had.

The door was ajar, so she took a step in his direction. Morgan spun around in his chair and gave her his passionate look. He patted his lap, indicating he wanted her to sit there. Kyna hesitated for only seconds before complying with his request.

"Who were you talking to?" Kyna asked once he ended the call.

"That was just business," Morgan tossed the phone on the desk.

"In Dubai again?" Kyna hated that she couldn't hide the jealous tinge to her voice. Even after their night, she felt like something wasn't right with him.

"Actually, New York. And before you ask, it was with an investor who keeps really late hours due to his headquarters being in Tokyo."

"Come back to bed," Kyna pleaded with him.

"I have some things I need to finish up. Give me a few minutes."

Kyna all but fell off his lap when he turned back to his laptop and starting looking at some kind of spreadsheet. "Whatever, not like I haven't slept alone before."

She didn't know where that attitude came from. Maybe it was the frustration of frequently waking in the middle of the night and finding her husband not beside her. They only saw one another on weekends. He would arrive on Friday and leave on Sunday. It wasn't even 48 hours because she had to attend church and continue going to family dinners to not raise suspicions around her.

Kyna's work schedule was getting busier with the women in her research program. Their pregnancies were coming to full term within weeks of each other. Mrs. McCarter had just delivered her triplets, and Mrs. Thomas was scheduled for a C-section the next week. Kyna wanted to spend as much time with her husband as possible. Especially since he had so little time to spare as well.

Often, she felt like a spoiled little girl who didn't get her way. She stalked away from the office and into the kitchen to find a snack. Opening the refrigerator, she found some celery and carrot sticks. A side of hummus would make this a healthy snack and a way to calm her nerves. When she couldn't find the hummus, she slammed the refrigerator door shut and turned smack dab into Morgan. He had been standing behind her while she fumed. She stared up into his dark, sexy eyes that appeared darker than usual.

So what if he was upset with her? She was angry, too. Maybe the secrecy was taking too much of a toll on her. And perhaps she should be more understanding that Morgan was doing the best he could. They lived in different states and had different types of workplace demands.

"Kyna, I have a company to run. If I don't work, we don't have money to fly all over the place."

He wasn't touching her. In the past, when they had disagreements, he would hold her, rub her arms or some type of affection. Now, he was standing there looking at her with an unrecognizable glare. "Did I ask you for all of these trips here and there? I distinctly remember telling you that you spend too much money," Kyna retorted.

"You don't seem to mind when you are buying clothes and shoes," Morgan countered.

"That was even beneath you, Husband."

Neither of them spoke for minutes, both seeming to size the other up. Kyna wanted to shrink under his gaze, but she refused to. Instead, she jutted her chin forward in a challenging way. Morgan didn't back down, either. Finally, Kyna broke their stare down and let out a slow, low breath.

"Come back to bed," she asked again.

"I have some more work to finish up. I will be there when I am finished."

"Whatever," Kyna left her snacks on the breakfast bar and went back to her room.

Morgan followed her to the bedroom and wrapped his arm around her waist. He pulled her flush against his body and whispered in her ear, "I know this secrecy is starting to wear on you. Please give me a few more weeks. I have a deal I am working on, and I need to stay focused. No interference from the media, our families, outside influences, nothing. This deal is important to me. It's important for us. Can you give me just a few more weeks?"

Kyna felt his love through his arms. She needed to feel his touch; when he did this, she knew everything would be okay. Unable to get past the lump in her throat to answer him, she reluctantly nodded her head in agreement.

When he was this close, her brain went haywire. At that moment, in his arms, she loved him so much that she would agree to almost anything he asked of her. That included keeping their marriage a secret a little while longer. They told each other it was just to get to know one another better, then it became exciting, now it was grating on her nerves. Not being able to talk to her sisters about her marriage and life, in general, was straining her relationship with them. Her sisters still didn't know about her doctorate degree. Kyna was sure they would go ballistic when they found out how much she had been hiding from them.

Chapter 9

Since the weekend, when Kyna had her mini-meltdown with Morgan, she hadn't seen him as much. It wasn't because of their disagreement, but both of their work schedules prevented them from being able to connect. Morgan still called every night, and their bible study remained the only constant in their relationship. She looked forward to that time with him because it often felt like that was when they connected the most.

Friday night would be the first weekend she had off in a month. Morgan was in China on business, and she had no desire to fly there for a day and have to fly back. Instead, she promised her friends they could hang out since they had not done that since her graduation celebration. Kyna met Chelsea and Alexis at the Vault, a nightclub that used to be a bank. The DJ had the dance floor packed when they arrived.

"Let's look to see whose VIP area we can sneak into tonight," Alexis said. That was how the three of them liked to party. Get dressed up and find some guys to let them into their private area. Otherwise, they would be standing the entire night, and that was not what any of them wanted while wearing four-inch heels. Aside from the bar area, the VIP sections were the only places in the club that had seating.

"Lex, we don't have to worry about that tonight. I took care of it," Kyna yelled over the loud music and nodded her head toward the VIP suites. Alexis and Chelsea followed behind her until they stopped at a small section roped off with her name on it.

"How much was bottle service? I want to give you something on it." Chelsea reached for her phone to electronically send money to Kyna.

"Put your phone away. I got this. Let's just have fun," Kyna grabbed a bottle of champagne and poured them each a glass.

The night was similar to all other nights. The ladies danced with anyone who asked and declined all drinks from random men. About midnight, Mario and Hunter joined the trio. Mario had been a nursing student with Kyna. They graduated and started at Memorial Hospital together. Mario left the hospital after a year to work for a visiting nurses group. He enjoyed the traveling aspect of the job and seeing the world without having to spend any of his money. Hunter was an imaging technician at Memorial. He was married with three kids, but his wife hated the clubs, so he hung out with the group from time to time.

"Honey, thank you for being so generous. I was not prepared to be knocked around at the bar all night." Mario leaned back, draping one arm across the back of the black leather sofa and using his free hand to twirl his favorite drink of cranberry juice and Crown Royal Apple. He was sitting close to Kyna so he could be heard over the music.

Kyna laughed at him. Whenever he drank a lot, he started calling everyone, "Honey."

"How many of those have you had?" Alexis asked Mario.

"Not enough to make you attractive."

That was another thing Kyna remembered about Mario when he drank too much; he was brutally honest. He and Alexis got along like oil and water. Alexis knew this also, which is why she ignored him most of the time. But tonight, she must have had one too many drinks herself.

"You ain't all that attractive, either. That's why you in here with us. You know this is a straight club, right?"

"It may be a straight club, but at least one of those dudes that you danced with looked my way. Be careful, Honey." He said the last sentence with a swirl of his glass in the air. Kyna was glad they just stared at each other and neither took their dramatics any further.

Kyna laughed at her friends; she loved them for their differing personalities. There was never a dull moment with any of them.

Just before last call, the ladies excused themselves to make a stop in the restroom. Kyna refreshed her make-up and reapplied her lip gloss. On her way back to the suite, she bumped into the last person she thought she would see again. He was tall and massively built like a football player. When she looked up, she was faced with a past she had long ago forgotten.

"Kyna, is that you?"

"Bruce," she replied dryly, hiding her shock. She attempted to walk away, but he blocked her path.

"Hey, you look good. What has it been, five years? Yeah, you look real good." He was eyeing her like she was a juicy steak. He even licked his lips, and that caused her stomach to turn over. Kyna didn't respond and tried to move around him, but he sidestepped her again.

"Let's get together soon. I would love to catch up with you."

"I don't think so," Kyna answered.

"Why? You got a man or something." He looked around to see if anyone was looking out for her.

"Or something." Kyna looked around, too, hoping to make eye contact with Mario or Hunter.

"Sounds like he not doing his job if he not here with you." Kyna took a step back. His breath reeked of a liquor store mixed with smelly cigars. He was right in her face, and the smell was causing her head to throb.

"I didn't say he wasn't here." Once again, she tried to walk away but couldn't.

"Well, I've been talking to you for a few minutes, and he ain't came over here. Yeah, you ain't got no man. Listen, I'll give you a call tomorrow. We can have dinner at the

Garrison." Bruce looked down at his cell phone like he was checking his calendar or something.

Kyna knew he was trying to flex for some reason. The Garrison was a very upscale restaurant that only took reservations, and the waitlist was at least a month long.

"You do that." She was finally able to get past him and walk to her suite.

When she got back to her party, Chelsea was the first to ask, "Who was that chunk of fine chocolate man?"

"His name is Bruce, and you can have him." Kyna couldn't remember why she had dated him in the first place. His ego was taller than most skyscrapers. As soon as she found out he liked to drop names to get girls to date him, she began ignoring his calls and texts. He eventually moved on to the next girl.

"Oh, Honey, we need to go somewhere and get something to eat. And you need to dish," Mario said.

"You guys fill me in later. I'm heading home," Hunter said.

"Yes, get home to the family. I forget you have a curfew," Mario responded.

"That I do. I get my little freedom, and all my wife asks is that I come home at a decent hour. Clubs close at 2 A.M., and I should be home by 2:30."

Kyna thought about what Hunter said for a minute. Morgan had been upset with her once when she stayed out all night. That prompted her to pull her phone from her purse and send him a text message. Kyna was sure that Jesse was somewhere nearby and was probably feeding Morgan a play-by-play of her evening. Yet, she wanted to let Morgan know she was okay and with friends.

After leaving the club, they all jumped into the car with Chelsea, and they headed to their favorite 24-hour restaurant, IHOP. There were a few other groups from the club in IHOP, but it was mostly quiet. Kyna checked her phone to see if Morgan had responded. She frowned when there was no message. Over the next hour, she checked her phone at least five more times and still no response.

"Who you checking for?" Alexis asked.

"What? No one." Kyna tossed her phone into her purse.

"Yeah, right. You've been checking that phone every 10 minutes. Who is he?" Chelsea asked.

Kyna didn't answer, but smiled at the thought of her secret. Then, she started thinking about how her friends would react when they found out. She didn't wear her wedding ring or any new jewelry that Morgan lavishly gifted her in public. It would draw too much attention.

"He must be fine if you are keeping him to yourself," Chelsea responded and sat back in her seat. She turned her head away, which was her way of letting you know she felt left out.

"Or she just doesn't want you heffas in her business," Mario responded.

"Who you calling a heffa?" Alexis raised her voice.

Kyna knew she had to put a stop to this. Cooler heads needed to prevail, and at the moment, neither of them had cooler heads. "Hey, both of you, stop. I don't know why you always starting stuff with her," Kyna directed her statement to Mario.

Instead of responding to Kyna, Mario rolled his eyes and turned away from the women. That was his way of telling Kyna he would stop for now.

There was a quiet moment among the group, each seeming to be in their own thoughts until Kyna's phone started buzzing in her bag. She quickly checked, hoping to see a message from Morgan. Instead, it was a text from Bruce. Kyna wondered how he got her phone number so quickly. The text was a confirmation that he had the right number. She chose not to respond.

"That must not be the text she was waiting for. Her whole face turned sour," Alexis commented.

"Let's talk about something else," Kyna placed the phone back in her bag.

"Yes, what's up with Dr. Hawkins?" Chelsea asked.

Kyna laughed. Chelsea had seen Grant once and got it in her head that she would seduce him into a date with her. Only one problem in her plan; Grant has never paid her any attention. Most of the time, he looked right through her when she came around. "Scratch that thought. He is sniffing behind my sister."

"Which one? Poe or Karmyn?" Chelsea asked.

"Can't be Poe; she stay busy with her real estate business. It must be Karmyn. She always in the gym wearing those tight gym clothes. I bet all the men be after her," Alexis interjected with a bit of envy.

"Maybe I should get a gym membership. She does have all those fine, rich men up in there. Working out and sweating," Chelsea started fanning herself.

"Honey, you can't afford Karmyn's gym. Now, Planet Fitness has $10 monthly memberships." Mario couldn't keep quiet for long. That comment got Alexis and Chelsea all riled up again.

Kyna took the check for their meals and went to pay the cashier. She wanted to leave before they started fighting. Unfortunately, she was about 10 seconds too late when Alexis grabbed the maple syrup and attempted to pour it over Mario's head. Mario took his plate, which still had eggs on it and blocked her hand. That caused Alexis to pour the syrup on Chelsea's new all-white leather pants. Chelsea jumped up, screaming at both of them.

That was Kyna's cue to leave them right there. She stepped outside to see if she could find Jesse. She knew he had to be there. Apparently, his skills at being covert were getting better. She couldn't find him, so she pulled out her phone and ordered a Lyft instead. Kyna felt slightly saddened that Morgan stopped Jesse from following her. She didn't want to admit it, but she took comfort in knowing that someone was looking out for her.

After tipping the driver, Kyna walked to her front door and stood there for a few seconds. The hairs on the back of her neck stood, and her heart plummeted. It was that feeling happening again. She promised herself she was moving into the condo the next time it happened. Kyna needed to tell

Morgan about what was happening. She would have to explain the sudden move into the condo anyway.

The area didn't show any strange signs, no one was outside at this time of the morning, and the area was well-lit. Brushing off the unusual feeling, she opened her door and reset her alarm. After taking two steps into the darkened room, suddenly it was flooded with light. Morgan was sitting on the sofa and scared Kyna half to death. He was becoming good at scaring her with his unexpected appearances.

*****

"Glad to see you know where home is," Morgan stated without looking in her direction.

"Morgan, you scared me. When did you get here? I thought you were out of the country," Kyna fumbled around, trying to catch her breath.

He twirled a glass of wine in his hand and took a sip before answering her. "I've been here for about an hour. Imagine how I felt when I got here, and you were not."

"I was out with friends. I sent you a text message. And I know Jesse is lurking somewhere."

"Well, I didn't get a text message." Morgan drained the contents of the glass in one gulp. Placing the glass on the table, he stood to his full height, seemingly too big for Kyna's apartment. He had been in her apartment many times, and only now did he seem to loom over everything. "You are right about one thing. Jesse was with you."

"So, you knew I was safe." Kyna attempted to walk past him into the kitchen. Morgan knew that she would try to retreat, but he wasn't about to let that happen. He blocked her path and reached out to hold her hands. He took a calming breath before continuing.

"Who were the men you were with tonight?" Morgan tried to school his features to be soft and gentle, but he was feeling anything but. He was angry. The 11-hour flight was brutal, but all he could think about was getting to his wife. The deal he just closed would net him a profit of over $65 million, and he wanted to share his accomplishment with her. Yet, she was out with friends, drinking and partying.

Kyna hitched an eyebrow and replied, "Friends."

"Friends? What are their names?" Morgan demanded with more force than necessary.

"What difference does it make?"

"Kyna, don't do that. I asked you a question."

"You're jealous." Kyna tried to free herself from his grasp, but that only caused him to tighten his grip. "We are better than this." She brought his attention to how he was holding her.

"Are we?" Morgan didn't loosen his grip. "My wife hanging out in a nightclub with two men, I don't know. Then, going to eat at the IHOP until almost five o'clock in the morning."

"Morgan, I can't do this right now, okay. Can we talk in the morning?"

"Kyna! It is morning." He finally released her, not sure what he would do next. "What do you want? Time to figure out what lie to tell me? I thought we promised to always be honest with one another, even if it might hurt the other person." Morgan took a step back and glared down at her. "Tell me now if you want out of this marriage."

"What? No! I love you, Morgan. That hasn't changed. Why would you think that?"

Morgan saw the fear and confusion leap into her eyes. Immediately, he regretted his words. He was jumping to conclusions, and that was guiding his thoughts. "We've been distant these last few weeks. And I can't help but think you want someone else. Especially when I see you cozied up with another man."

"What are you talking about?"

"I called Jesse when I landed. He told me where you were. I came up to the IHOP and saw you wrapped up with that guy."

"You misinterpreted what you saw. Mario bats for the other team. He is not into women."

Morgan dropped his jaw and now felt utterly embarrassed. He was talking to her about trust, yet he didn't trust her. Now he was having to apologize for jumping the gun. But, when he tried to speak, the words didn't come out. What could he say to her? He could get on his knees and grovel, beg for her forgiveness. Even now, she wasn't making this easy for him. She stood there with her arms crossed over her chest and tapping her foot. "I'm sorry for jumping to conclusions. It's just that I expected you..."

"You expected me to be here waiting for you to return home." Kyna used the back of her hand to wipe away a stray tear. "We can't keep doing this. Morgan, the separation, it's starting to wear on me and you, too."

Morgan's heart tore into pieces as he heard her words. He couldn't give her what he knew she wanted deep down. Having their secret finally come to light would lessen a lot of what they were feeling. The strain of living separately was creating too many jealousy fueled accusations between them. Once this last contract deal was signed, Morgan promised he would yell from the rooftops how much he loved his wife. Nothing would stop him from telling the world.

"I know, Queen." He reached for her again, wanting to comfort her. When she didn't withdraw, he pulled her closer. "We knew that this could happen when we agreed to keep our marriage a secret. I just need a few more weeks. This deal I am working on is almost done."

"Morgan, you said that a few weeks ago. Now, we have been married for nearly six months. Do you know how difficult this is to keep secrets from my sisters?"

"Have you told them about your doctorate degree?"

"No, but that's different."

Morgan guided them into the kitchen. The sun was beginning to rise, and he figured they may be awake for some time. Even though he had been drinking before Kyna arrived home, Morgan needed a cup of coffee to focus on the conversation they were having.

"How is it different, Kyna? You are still keeping secrets from your family. All I'm asking is for time to close this deal. Then, I will be able to focus on nothing but you and our marriage."

They both heard a buzzing noise off into the distance. Neither wanted to acknowledge the sound, but when it broke into the room's silence again, both went in search of their cell phones. Morgan found his phone first and found there were no messages. He looked over to Kyna, watched her glance at her phone, and then tossed it back into her purse.

"Who was that?" he asked.

"No one." Kyna walked back into the kitchen and pulled two coffee mugs from the cabinet.

Morgan didn't want to make a big deal of anything. But, he was concerned about her. "It was someone, or else you wouldn't have scowled the way that you did."

"It was an ex-boyfriend I ran into at the club. He asked me to dinner. I wish I could have told him I was married," Kyna responded, voice still loaded with attitude.

Morgan wanted to know who this ex-boyfriend was. He wanted to know why this guy thought it was okay to text Kyna at five in the morning. The facial reaction she gave when she saw his message led Morgan to believe she was not interested in him. So, for the moment, he let the issue slide. But, later in the day, he would have Jesse check into things.

Instead of dwelling on something he could not change and a subject Kyna clearly did not want to discuss, Morgan tried to smooth things over with the promise of a vacation.

"Kyna, please. A couple of more weeks. Then, I will take you on a vacation like you have never had. Just me and you in Fiji."

She dropped her arms from across her chest and sighed, "Morgan, it's never been about the money, the trips, or the jewelry. Why aren't you listening? I only want you," Kyna implored.

They were at a stalemate. Morgan noticed Kyna was unstable, still standing in her heels. She had been partying all night. The coffee could wait until later. He gently lifted her into his arms and carried her to bed. She needed to get some sleep, and he needed to think.

The next afternoon, Morgan was awake and having a cup of coffee in the kitchen. Kyna went right to sleep after their heated discussion that morning. He didn't want to call it an argument, but they did need more time to talk.

Morgan took another sip of coffee and reached for his laptop when he heard buzzing coming from nearby. He looked around and found Kyna's phone on the sofa. It must have fallen out when she tossed her purse down. Morgan grabbed the phone and read the text messages. One was from her mother, and three were from someone named Bruce.

The first text message was confirming dinner at the Garrison for next Friday night. The second text was an apology for their past relationship. And the third text message was a picture of the man without a shirt. Morgan's anger increased as he read each message. The image put him over the edge. He immediately found his phone and made a call. Bruce must be the ex-boyfriend who texted her earlier. He was going to regret ever reaching out to Kyna.

Kyna didn't wake until well into the afternoon. Morgan had been in the spare bedroom, hunched over his computer and didn't hear Kyna wake or enter the room.

"How long are you going to work this weekend?" Kyna asked.

"I was waiting for you to wake up," Morgan closed his laptop.

"Well, I'm awake now." Kyna cocked her head to the side.

"Let's eat. I ordered Italian from Angelo's." Morgan led her into the kitchen and removed two metal pans from the oven. They remained silent while he plated their food, allowing the sounds of nature to fill the room. Morgan grabbed her hands and blessed the food. After taking one forkful of his rigatoni, he asked the question he didn't want the answer to.

"Are you attracted to him?"

Kyna popped her head up and asked, "Attracted to who?"

"Bruce," Morgan flatly said.

"Bruce? My ex-boyfriend? Why would you ask that question?"

"Because he asked you to dinner, and this morning he confirmed your dinner plans and sent you a rather risqué picture of himself." Morgan pushed another forkful of his food into his mouth and intently watched Kyna.

"Where is my phone?" Morgan placed the phone in her hand and held it there for a few seconds before she yanked her hand away. As she scrolled through her messages, he observed her reactions. "I did not accept his dinner invitation, and I did not ask for this picture. Bruce is arrogant and a braggart. He enjoys tossing around that he is successful and believes that every woman should fall at his feet because he has shown them any interest." Kyna tossed her phone on the table.

"What were you attracted to?" Morgan continued his questioning.

"He wasn't always that way. In undergrad, he had some redeeming qualities. They just seemed to falter away after time."

Morgan remained silent for a while as they ate their meal. He didn't want to think of his wife with another man, even if it was her past. Morgan cleared the table and started the dishes. With his back to Kyna, he had no idea what she was doing or thinking.

"Morgan, I just sent a message to Bruce that I was not going to dinner with him and to stop texting me. I also blocked his number."

"You didn't have to do that. I trust you."

"Then what was all of that earlier? You were acting like a jealous man, again."

"Kyna, the time when we are not together, I worry about you. I should be here to take you out and keep men away from you." He reached out to her, and she hesitated before stepping into his embrace. "I've never done this before. Marriage, long-distance relationship, it's new, okay? We have to put in the work."

Kyna

Chapter 10

Morgan was in his office in New York, awaiting his sister's arrival. They were scheduled to have a conference call with John. John was still on-site at another location. It had been three weeks since Morgan last saw his wife. Once again, their schedules were conflicting, and not seeing one another was causing a great divide between them. Their nightly bible studies decreased due to his nightly meetings with investors overseas and Kyna's research study picking up pace. Many of the women who participated in the study were delivering their babies within days of each other.

The meeting Morgan was about to have with his siblings was to discuss finalizing the deal he had been working tirelessly on for several weeks. If all things went well, The Hawkins Group would triple their net worth, putting their entire family, firmly into the billionaire bracket. He had promised Kyna that they would go public with their marriage once he completed the deal, and he intended to keep his promise.

Melissa walked into Morgan's office and caught him smiling. He was remembering some of the good moments he and Kyna had at the beginning of their marriage. Then he thought, they were still at the beginning of their marriage.

"What did I do to you?" Melissa asked, taking her seat at the small conference table in Morgan's office.

"Why would you ask that?" Morgan gathered his files and joined her at the table.

"Because, you were smiling real big when I walked in, and now you are frowning."

Morgan smirked, "It's not you. I was just thinking of some work I have to do."

"I suppose." She gave him a disbelieving look. "Let's see if John is on time today." Morgan lowered the projector screen and logged into the online meeting room.

"He's been doing better coming to meetings in a timely manner," Morgan laughed. Melissa rolled her eyes, giving Morgan that same disbelieving look. John was never on time for meetings, but he somehow got the job done. Their mother often joked that John would be late for his own funeral.

"While we wait for John, how have you been? Seeing anyone?" Morgan asked.

"Wow, you sound like Mom. I'm dating here and there, but no one exclusively," Melissa answered.

"What happened to that dude from Jamaica?" Melissa had been dating a guy she met while vacationing in Jamaica. A few of her girlfriends wanted to see if they could be like Stella and get their groove back with some Jamaican youngsters.

"He found out who I was and wanted me to help him start his Jamaican restaurant. And by help, I mean he wanted me to finance it. Why do these men see me as a way to come up?"

"Melissa, you are the face of The Hawkins Group. They see you and know they have nothing to offer you. Don't worry, the right guy won't want money from you or a come-up. He is going to love you for you and not what you have." That message was more for himself than it was for Melissa.

Their meeting began when John's face appeared on the screen. After two hours of reviewing pages of contracts, Morgan was drained. Melissa was preparing to leave his office when Raven entered.

"Mr. Hawkins, do not forget you are attending the party at the Conley estate this evening. I placed your tuxedo in the closet in case you want to dress from here," Raven said.

"Thank you, Raven." Morgan noticed she was about to say something else, but cut her eyes to Melissa, smiled and closed the door behind her.

"So, you're going to Raymond Conley's party?" Melissa said it as a question and not a statement.

"I should make you go. There will be plenty of wealthy single men there. None of them will want you for your money or connections," Morgan laughed at his sister. She hated rubbing elbows with other rich people. Even though her job was to do that very thing. Whenever she could get out of attending an event, she would do so.

"I would be bored to death in five minutes. I would rather watch paint dry. Have a good weekend, brother."

Morgan roared this time. He couldn't wait until the day when some man got through her wall of defenses. She was going to fall hard, and he was going to enjoy watching it.

Raymond Conley was hosting yet another fundraiser for some politician Morgan didn't care about. These events were for current and future senators and congressmen to meet with the wealthiest people of New York. Morgan accepted the invitation at the request of Bridget before he met Kyna. Now, he wasn't remotely interested in being in the same room with the obnoxious socialite. Unfortunately, he confirmed his attendance, and he had no choice but to make an appearance.

The Conley mansion was massive and reminded Morgan of the Von Trapp house from the movie, *The Sound of Music*. He actually overheard someone say the home's original builder loved the movie so much he wanted one for himself.

Morgan moved about the room, speaking with this person and that person, attempting to avoid the very person who stood before him. Bridget was overly made up and wore a dress that hugged every curve she didn't have. He found nothing attractive about her figure. Kyna was small but shapely. She had curves for miles. Morgan was envisioning his wife when Bridget's voice broke into his thoughts.

"Morgan, I'm so glad you could make it. Didn't you bring your little pop-tart?"

Morgan remembered what Kyna said to him the last time they encountered Bridget. He lowered his voice, but kept the anger out. "Bridget, name-calling is beneath you."

She ignored his retort and continued, "Well, I'm glad she is old news because I have someone for you to meet."

Morgan let Bridget think whatever she wanted to. In due time, everyone will know the truth. Bridget waved her hand across, grabbing the attention of a young lady to join them. She was tall and thin, probably a model. The first thing Morgan noticed was the woman's eyelashes. He knew women added lashes for length and thickness, but her lashes reminded Morgan of a bird ready for take-off. She kept batting them in an attempt to appear demure.

"Morgan, this is my college friend, Daneida Bell. She is a journalist in Philadelphia. I'm trying to convince her to come back home." Bridget was grinning, looking back and forth between Morgan and Daneida.

Morgan did not want to appear rude, and honestly, talking to her may be better than talking to some of the stiff jackets in the room. "It is a pleasure to meet you. Are you from New York?"

"Queens, Jamaica Estates. We moved around growing up, but I call Philly home now. What about you?"

Bridget interrupted and smiled, "Well, I will leave you two to get acquainted."

After Bridget walked away, leaving the two of them standing together, they both laughed. "Bridget thinks she is a matchmaker. She hasn't been successful since I met her," Daneida said.

Morgan kept looking at the journalist and wondered how she would look once she removed the lashes, eyebrows and pounds of contouring foundation. She seemed to have a great personality.

The two conversed for a few minutes before being approached by Raymond Conley. He had been making his way around the room. Morgan knew it was just a matter of time before he got to them.

"Morgan, glad you could make it. I see you have met WPHL's number 1 investigative reporter." Raymond had a drink in one hand and used the other to reach out to Morgan for a handshake.

Morgan accepted his hand. "Raymond, happy to be here. And yes, Ms. Bell and I have met, although she didn't tell me she was an investigative reporter."

"Well, be careful of this one. She is very good at her job," Raymond patted him on the back before welcoming Howard Lewis, a candidate for U.S. Senate, to their group.

"Ah, Howard, please, come meet Morgan Hawkins of The Hawkins Group. Morgan, this is our next New York Senator," Raymond made the introductions.

Howard smiled and reached for Morgan's hand. Morgan thought the man was young to be running for senator, and a bit too eager. He smiled too big, and his eyes darted back and forth quickly. He appeared nervous and uncomfortable in his surroundings. In good measure, Morgan took his hand in a firm handshake.

"Pleased to meet you, sir. I have heard quite a few good things about The Hawkins Group."

"It's a pleasure to meet you. The Hawkins Group has a few good things going on," Morgan replied.

Before anyone else could speak, a photographer came over to take a picture of the group. Morgan tried to step away from Daneida, but she grabbed his hand and pulled him closer. In the back of his mind, Morgan knew he would have to explain that picture if it ever made it to Kyna.

"Mr. Hawkins, thank you for attending, and I hope I can count on your support come November," Howard smiled again.

"We will see." Morgan did not commit to supporting the young man. He would need to do a considerable amount of research before publicly backing any candidate.

For the remainder of the evening, Morgan couldn't seem to shake Daneida. Anytime he walked away, she was right back by his side. To the outsider looking in, they appeared to be a couple. By the end of the night, several people mentioned how great they looked together. If only they knew the truth.

And the truth was eating away at him all evening, even into the next morning. Morgan was never going to grow any closer to his wife if he didn't make their marriage publicly known. If women were continuing to come on to him, he was sure Kyna was still attracting men without being able to tell them she was married.

Morgan thought about the last few months since marrying Kyna. At first, they wanted to get to know each other without outside influences, mainly their families. Then, Morgan wanted to wait for his current business deal to finalize. Now that the deal was close to finalization, he would be able to help Kyna plan their coming out party.

The next morning, he arrived at the office with a smile on his face but a grim internal feeling. Morgan looked around and noticed staff looking at him under veiled hesitation. Raven greeted him from her desk.

"Good morning, Mr. Hawkins."

"Good morning, Raven. What is going on around here? Did I miss something?" Morgan grabbed his morning file from her desk and proceeded into his office.

Raven waited for Morgan to be seated behind his desk before shoving a handful of newspapers into his hands. "Everyone seems to be talking about this."

The first newspaper showed the picture of Conley, Morgan, Daneida, and Howard Lewis with a headline, "Hawkins Throws His Support Behind Lewis." That made Morgan angry. The next paper was a trashy tabloid that said, "Billionaire Playboy Finally Shows Signs of Settling Down With News Reporter Daneida Bell."

Morgan crumpled the papers and tossed them in the trash can next to his desk. The nerve of these people to print blatant lies about him. He hated frivolous lawsuits, but maybe his attorneys could make a case for liable. He needed to talk to his sister.

"Mr. Hawkins, I have already called Melissa and Daniel to the conference room." Daniel Dugan was a corporate fixer and was very successful in changing the narrative to fit his client's needs.

"Thank you, Raven. Please let them know I will be there in 10 minutes." Raven nodded and closed his office door.

This was another obstacle he and Kyna would have to face together. Morgan had just made the decision that they would announce their marriage within the next month. It seems the decision was being taken from him. If he had to choose his company over his wife, she would win every time.

Before he could talk to his sister and Daniel, he needed to speak with Kyna first. He tried to call her, but there was no answer on her cell phone or at her office. Morgan was sure she had seen at least one of those papers. He rationalized that it had to be the reason she was not answering his call. On his way to the conference room, Morgan instructed Raven to keep trying to reach Kyna.

Melissa and Daniel had been discussing something quietly when Morgan entered the conference room. They were head to head, leaning over a document that Daniel quickly put away when he saw Morgan.

"Good morning," Morgan addressed them.

"Nothing good about this," Melissa responded. "Have you seen the papers?"

"It's all lies," Morgan casually answered and took a seat at the table.

"Which part?" Melissa tossed a sheet of paper toward him. It appeared to have been a printout from a gossip site on the internet.

Morgan looked over the information and inwardly cringed. He managed to keep his real emotions intact. The article implicated that Morgan had been sleeping around with an unknown woman while courting Daneida Bell. There was a picture taken of him and Kyna at Dollywood when they visited Pigeon Forge. Kyna's face was mostly covered by her huge sunglasses and a big hat. If her sisters, or anyone else who knew Kyna, looked close enough, they would know it was her. He had to talk to her as soon as possible.

"Daniel, I don't need to tell you that this is serious. Especially since it is all lies. I met Ms. Bell last night for the first time. I need you to take care of this and also dig a little further into the picture."

"Who is she?" Melissa asked, pointing to the photo in the printout.

The time to tell his sister the truth was now. As the head of public relations, she needed to know everything. "This does not leave this room." Morgan paused, then took a deep breath before continuing. "The woman in the photo is Kyna Hammond–Hawkins. She is my wife."

Melissa came to her feet, then sat down for a second before jumping to her feet again. "Morgan, what have you done? We don't need this type of publicity with so much on the line. These investors are crazy religious. Don't you remember, they didn't want to deal with us because we were single. They could nix the whole deal. We are days from finalizing the current project, and next week is the groundbreaking for the new hotel."

Angrily, Morgan stood and dropped his fist onto the table, "Melissa, don't you think I know this? We didn't plan for our relationship to come out until after the deal was done."

Melissa and Morgan were in a staring battle. Finally, Melissa broke the intense eye battle of wills and asked, "When did you get married?"

"A few months ago."

"Months? Who else knows?" Melissa angrily asked.

"Just Raven, and now the two of you." Morgan returned to his chair and watched Melissa, who was now pacing the room.

"Raven knows. Of course, she knows. She knows everything about my brother before I do." Melissa gazed at Morgan with a look of remorse. She regretted the words as soon as they left her mouth. Morgan knew his sister was often concerned that she knew so little about his personal life.

Daniel took this opportunity to exit the room before they did or said something he didn't need to hear. "I think I will leave you two alone. Morgan, I am already on this."

"Thank you, Daniel." Morgan waited for him to close the door as he left the conference room, then he returned his attention to his sister, who was still steaming mad. "Melissa, please sit down. Let me tell you everything."

Morgan spent the past hour telling his sister how he met Kyna and their whirlwind love affair up to the day. While she processed the information being said to her, Raven slipped into the room and handed Morgan a note. The note simply said Kyna asked that you give her time.

Morgan felt a piercing through his heart. He wasn't sure what Kyna was thinking. She had to know he would never cheat on her. She had to trust him, or their marriage was never going to survive. Whoever was behind this lie, he was going to have their head for it.

Melissa had left Morgan's office, still upset about not knowing what was going on in his life. At least she understood why he wanted to keep his marriage a secret, especially with the business deal to finalize soon. Morgan had gotten his sister to a place where she wasn't screaming at him anymore. Often, Melissa questioned her siblings and demanded answers like she were the oldest, then times like now, when she acted like the youngest by threatening to tell their parents.

Morgan flipped the note between his fingers, over and over again. He wanted to respect Kyna's wishes but knew he needed to talk to her. He picked up the phone to dial her number but instead just stared at the phone. Words held very little weight in their relationship. Releasing some tension would help his decision-making. Maybe a few rounds in the boxing ring would help.

*****

Kyna had been online looking for an anniversary gift to give to her husband. He had been so understanding of her roller coaster of emotions. Their separation was beginning to wear on her mental capacity. She was tired of hiding her relationship and tired of lying to her sisters. She really wanted to let the world know that she was married and how wonderful her husband was.

Her online search for the perfect gift led her to an entertainment website, 21 Gifts Stars Gave Their Spouses. She thought the idea was intriguing and clicked on the first photo only to find a story about Morgan in the side news.

Kyna clicked on the image showing Morgan and a woman that she did not know. The headline insinuated that Morgan was in a relationship with this woman. As Kyna continued to read, she became angrier and angrier, allowing her jealous side to surface again. With each click of the mouse, she became more infuriated. This woman was a reporter and has been to several of the same events Morgan attended in the past year.

The ringtone for Raven briefly brought Kyna out of her cloud of anger. She wasn't in the right frame of mind to accept the call, so she grabbed her phone and hung up. Raven attempted to call back, again and again. Instead of directing her anger at the woman who had nothing to do with this situation, Kyna simply blocked the call and sent a text message to Raven; *Please let Morgan know I just need time.*

Looking at her apartment, where she and Morgan had many memories over the past few months, increased her sadness. Kyna locked up her apartment, jumped in her car and headed north to nowhere in particular. Before she realized where she was going, Kyna was in front of Alexis house. When Alexis opened the door, Kyna couldn't stop crying. Everything going on in her life was overwhelming, and Kyna needed to tell somebody. She needed to talk.

"I can't believe I believed everything he said. A handsome, successful, and obscenely rich man wouldn't want a simple nurse like me." Kyna grabbed at the tissue box Alexis was holding.

"How could you say that?" Alexis said. "You are one of the most intelligent women I know. You are beautiful on the inside, as well as, the outside. Any man, no matter how much money he has, would want to be with you. I think that is what Morgan saw in you on the first night."

"What do you know about the first night?" Kyna asked after blowing her nose loudly into the tissue. "You were not there. Remember, you left at the end of the party."

"I didn't leave," Alexis shyly admitted. "I watched the man at the bar longer than you did. He kept glancing over at us. And when we ended the party, I met up with Michael in the garden, and we saw you two."

Kyna was shocked at what her friend just revealed. Not only that she was seeing her ex-boyfriend Michael again, but also that she and Morgan were not alone in the garden. She wanted to question her best friend about keeping secrets, but that would make her the stone in the glass house.

"What about the next day at the spa? Why didn't you say anything?" Kyna asked. "You must have known that it was Morgan who paid for everything."

"What was I supposed to say? If I said anything, I would have had to tell you about Michael. I didn't want you or anyone else to know that I was seeing Michael again. Remember, we had broken up, and you were the one who told me not to go back to him. I didn't want to hear you or Chelsea passing judgment on me."

Kyna remembered the days when Alexis would show up on her doorstep, crying about something Michael had done. Now, the tables were turned, and Kyna was now crying on

Alexis' shoulder. When she couldn't go to her sisters, Alexis was always there to fill the void.

"Let me ask you a question. Do you really believe in your heart that Morgan cheated on you?" Alexis asked.

Kyna was not sure what to believe anymore. The picture and the article in the tabloid were questionable. But, it was a tabloid website not known for its reliable sources. And, to Morgan's credit, he had called her earlier that morning. Then Raven called several times. They must have been trying to get to her before she had a chance to see it for herself.

Before Kyna could respond, Alexis continued, "Just so I understand, the magazine with the picture is not reputable, yet you are all upset and thinking he has cheated when he has never given you a reason to believe this. It's time you stop living in the past. Morgan is not like any of your ex-boyfriends. He is a man of integrity, and you know it." Alexis jabbed Kyna in the chest.

"How do you know he is a man of integrity?" Kyna wanted to know how her friend could make such an assumption about someone she had never met.

"I recognized his name from somewhere. So, my untrustworthy nature caused me to do a background check on him. Seems he is more than just a single billionaire or was single. He has a really giving heart and spirit that I think matches yours as well." Alexis smiled.

Kyna had read the same information about Morgan from her internet search. That was one of the reasons why she loved him so much, because he was not a boaster. Often times he gave from his heart, not wanting any recognition for his actions.

Kyna and Alexis sat there for a few more hours and talked. She still wasn't ready to talk to Morgan. He had put himself in the position to be photographed with this unknown woman. Kyna just wanted to go somewhere quiet and pray about the decisions she had made. Maybe they did jump into a marriage too soon. That question always lingered in the back of her mind anytime things were not perfect. No marriage was perfect, and this was the proof that theirs was far from it.

Instead of going back to her apartment, Kyna made her way to the riverfront, where she and Morgan had their first date. She sat on the same bench that they shared and looked out onto the water, reflecting on the past few months of her life and how they took this crazy turn. They had good intentions before her irrational fears, and their shared jealousy caused them both to second guess the other.

Kyna had gone from doctoral student graduate to married woman in one weekend. Funny how you make plans for your life, and God laughs. She truly understood that statement now. Never in her wildest dreams did she think she would be married. Decisions needed to be made about what she wanted in her life. Yet, nothing was coming to mind.

Talking to Morgan was the right thing to do, but she just couldn't do it right now. He would be in town for the groundbreaking ceremony of his new hotel. Until then, she would go home and pray and fast and pray again until she figured out what to do. Prayerfully, by then, she would know what to do.

A few hours later, Kyna wasn't surprised when she received a call from her sister. Kaleigh expressed to her family that this groundbreaking ceremony for The Hawkins Group was a significant accomplishment for her small realty company. She wanted her family in attendance to support her. Asking was futile; of course, her family would be there to support.

"Hey sis, what have you been up to? I haven't heard from you in a few weeks," Kaleigh inquired.

Kyna wanted to be honest and tell her sister everything. Why was it more comfortable to talk to Alexis and not her own sister? "I've been busy with work," Kyna stilled her voice, trying to keep the trembling to an unnoticeable level.

"Don't forget that the Hawkins family will be in town tomorrow, and the groundbreaking ceremony is on this Friday. I really want you to be there with me," Kaleigh continued.

"As long as my schedule permits, I will be there. I don't foresee there being any reason I can't make it." Kyna tapped the steering wheel with her thumb, a method she used to keep calm. Tears were welling up, and she was finding it difficult to keep them from falling.

Kyna changed the focus and asked her sister about her health. Kaleigh had been having some serious health issues recently. Several trips to the doctor and a couple of trips to the emergency room left Kaleigh with a bag of unanswered questions.

"I have my good days and bad days," her sister responded.

"So, the doctors still haven't told you what's wrong?"

"Nothing so far. I'm still waiting for a few more test results to come back."

Being a nurse, Kyna wanted to do more for her sister, but her specialty was reproduction and obstetrics. Kaleigh never liked to talk about herself and changed the subject to Dr. Grant Hawkins and how he was insistent on pursuing her. While her sister talked, Kyna had visions of Morgan. He looked so much like his brother, making it challenging to work beside Grant. A few times, she found herself staring at Grant, noticing the similarities between the two.

Groundbreaking day arrived, and Kyna was nervous about being in her husband's presence. How would she get through the morning? She was sure that if anyone were around them for more than a few seconds, they would know something was going on. Raven had sent a few text messages, making sure she was okay. Kyna wasn't sure if Morgan had told her to do it or if Raven was checking on her out of pure concern.

Kyna alternated between three outfits and decided to wear one of her designer, original jumpsuits and Jimmy Choo heels. She was assured that she wouldn't need to walk in any dirt, which could ruin her $1200 shoes. She pulled her hair tightly into a chignon at the nape of her neck and chose not to wear any jewelry. All of this primping and preparing was to look good for her husband. After hours of praying and crying, Kyna was prepared to see Morgan.

The assigned parking lot was full, including many local and national news stations. Kyna saw her sisters near the VIP tent. Thanks to Kaleigh, they all had access to the area. From afar, Kyna watched the Hammonds family and the Hawkins' family easily interacting with one another. And that was the way it should be. She just wished they knew they were in-laws. Kyna assumed the older woman was Morgan's mother, and the beautiful woman with her was Melissa, his sister. Instead of immediately joining her family, Kyna decided to stand back and observe everything.

The ceremony was fantastic and well planned. Kyna was so proud of her sister. She may have been the small fish in this deal, but this venture may have never taken off without her current real estate market expertise. Kyna took a deep breath, closed her eyes and prepared herself to face Morgan when she heard a disturbance near the dais.

Grant was dragging a woman away from the others. Kyna had a run-in with that woman at the hospital last week. Morgan would have to wait. Kaleigh needed her more. She was headed toward her sister when Morgan briefly made eye contact with her before asking Kaleigh to talk privately. They moved away from the crowd into the building.

"This day was going great until Carl Atwater showed up," Karleigh said.

"And who was that woman with Grant?" Karmyn asked.

Kyna approached the sisters, answering Karmyn's question. "She was at the hospital a few days ago. Apparently, she was engaged to Grant and now wants him back."

The sisters kept their eyes in the direction where Morgan and John took Kaleigh. A few minutes later, Kaleigh ran from the building, and that put the sisters in motion to give the Hawkins brothers a piece of their mind, with Kyna leading the charge.

Chapter 11 - Present Day

Kyna sat beside Morgan in the restaurant and allowed him to kiss her tears away. The only problem was, she had more tears than they had time. Her body was betraying her by craving his touch. If she didn't get out of this restaurant and into some fresh air, she would melt on the spot.

"Not here, OK?" She whispered, "We can go to our spot." Kyna rushed from the table, hoping he knew the place she was referring to. She needed a moment to get herself together.

They arrived at the waterfront at the same time, and walked in silence to the same bench where they spent their first date.

During the drive, Kyna was able to muster enough strength to stop crying. Once seated, she looked at him and really took in his features. His face was clean-shaven but noticeably thinner than the last time they were together. She could tell he hadn't been sleeping well. His eyes looked tired. She wondered if stress had anything to do with his condition.

"I do remember our first date," Kyna told him. "We sat here all night and talked." After a considerable amount of silence, she continued. "I missed you too. These last few weeks have been horrible for me. I prayed, and I cried, and I prayed some more. I talked to God, and I asked him to help me understand. What I found out was that maybe we did move too fast." She looked into his eyes and could see his heartbreaking. A single tear escaped his eye and ran down his cheek. She lost her cool and stopped him before he could say anything.

"I can't do this right now." Kyna stood quickly and raced away before Morgan could stop her.

She ran to her car and pulled away before Morgan could catch up to her. Kyna didn't want to give him a chance to smooth talk her into staying and talking. Her emotions were already erratic, and she needed someone to calm her down; she needed her sisters.

It took Kyna 30 minutes to get to Karmyn's house. She lived the closest of her sisters. Karmyn lived in a large house in Washington Heights. An upscale neighborhood where the most influential people in the city lived. Karmyn was able to keep the house that she and her ex-husband, NFL star Vincent Gallagher owned in her divorce settlement. Once Kyna cleared the security gate, she proceeded to her sister's house and noticed an unknown car in the driveway. She hoped Karmyn didn't have company, but she didn't care.

Kyna needed to talk to her sister. Kyna parked next to the unknown vehicle, took a deep breath, and jumped out of the car, racing to her sister's front door.

Kyna banged on the door like her life depended on it. After a few seconds, Karmyn answered the door pulling her robe together and tightening her belt.

"Sister? What's wrong? Why are you here this late?" Karmyn asked.

"I need to talk to you. I need to talk to you tonight." Kyna allowed the tears she had been holding in to flow freely.

Karmyn opened the door for Kyna to enter. "Are you okay? Has anything happened to you?"

"Everything has happened." Kyna walked through her sister's enormous house, into the kitchen, grabbed a bottle of water, and sat at the breakfast bar. Karmyn followed and sat on the opposite side.

"Talk to me. Tell me, what's going on with you?" She handed her sister a paper towel to wipe her tears.

"You are never going to believe this, but I did something so crazy and reckless, and now it has come back to bite me in the butt." Kyna looked around the room, not wanting to make direct contact with her sister. She took a swig of water and continued, "Six months ago, I got married."

Karmyn jumped up and yelled, "You did what? To who?"

"I married Morgan Hawkins."

There was a long silence before Karmyn sat down and spoke. "Don't stop now. Tell me the whole story."

Kyna told her sister everything, not leaving anything out. She needed advice; she needed someone to talk to. Karmyn sat there, staring at her sister, jaw hanging open. The silence was deafening. Kyna started fidgeting with her hands under the table, still unable to look at her sister. She was getting anxious because she had no idea what her sister was thinking.

"Sister, please, say something. I need you to tell me what to do," Kyna muttered.

"I don't know what to tell you. I have so many thoughts running through my mind. But, the only thing I see is that you truly love Morgan. Just listening to you talk, I can hear the love in your voice. I don't think you ever gave him a chance."

Kyna thought about what her sister said. Did she give him a chance, or did she go into this marriage, expecting it to fail? From the beginning, they talked about the difficulty of keeping things a secret and living apart. So why was she so upset?

Karmyn broke into her thoughts, "He's a billionaire, for Heaven's sake. Of course, women are going to come on to him. He is a target for the gold diggers of the world." She held Kyna's hands in hers. "Sister, you have to develop a thick skin and trust in your husband. Without trust, your marriage doesn't have a leg to stand on. A lesson learned from my failed marriage."

Kyna thought more about what her sister was saying. More questions to be answered. Did she truly trust Morgan? There were more questions than answers, and Kyna was still as confused as before. In the silence, Kyna heard a noise coming from somewhere in the house.

"Sister, is someone else here? I saw the car in the driveway." Kyna looked at her sister for the first time and saw Karmyn's cheeks turn red.

"Don't worry about that. It's just a friend visiting," Karmyn dismissed the question.

"A guy friend? I should have asked when I first arrived. I'm sorry to have intruded. I should leave." Kyna stood to leave.

Karmyn came around the breakfast bar and stopped her sister. "Sister, you are always welcome in my house no matter the day or time. You do not have to leave."

A sister's love was one Kyna would forever be grateful for. This conversation could have gone in several different directions. She was prepared for her sister to be angry, but only received her love and support.

"You have given me a lot to think about. I think I need to go home and pray some more."

Karmyn gave her a tight hug, holding on for a time longer than necessary. When she released Kyna, she asked, "How about this, I get Karleigh and Poe together, and we meet for breakfast in the morning?"

Telling her other sisters everything was inevitable. Informing their parents would be catastrophic. The sooner, the better. It didn't make sense to postpone the unavoidable.

"I think breakfast sounds great. We can meet at the Double Egg," Kyna suggested their favorite breakfast restaurant.

"I love you, sister. Whatever you decide, I will be here for you," Karmyn embraced her again.

"I love you, too." They walked arm in arm to the front door. "Maybe at breakfast, you will tell us who is upstairs. But for now, I promise to keep your secret."

"I'm not telling you or anyone else who is upstairs," Karmyn laughed before closing the door after Kyna was safely inside of her car.

Kyna felt better after confessing to her sister. She may not have gotten the advice she was looking for, but she received more matters to think about and questions she needed to answer. If she were honest with herself, she would have to admit that she did trust Morgan emphatically. Knowing that only led to more questions.

*****

The crisp, evening air whipped around Morgan as he sat on the bench absently watching the water ripple in the river. This was not the end of his marriage. He knew exactly where they went wrong, and it wasn't rushing into getting married. That was the one thing he was sure of. He was also convinced that Kyna still loved him, and that is why she was acting erratic and confused. Now, he had to come up with a plan to get her to understand she could trust him and trust his love for her.

Morgan sat on the bench, thinking until his cell phone rang. He didn't immediately recognize the number and almost sent the caller to voicemail. A feeling told him to answer. The security company servicing Kyna's apartment called to inform him that there had been a break-in. The representative couldn't finish his statement before Morgan started questioning him.

Luckily, no one was home at the time of the break-in. Morgan was grateful that Kyna did not go home after she left him. After making sure that the police were on their way, Morgan informed Jesse they needed to get to her apartment in record time. He was grateful Kyna's apartment wasn't far from the riverfront.

They arrived before the police, which angered Morgan. Not that he had much influence, but he would have a conversation with the mayor. The front door of the apartment was kicked in, and the place was ransacked. Pictures were yanked from the walls, furniture was flipped over, and dishes smashed onto the floor.

Who would do this to her? What motive did they have? Morgan closed his eyes and quickly said a prayer thanking God that Kyna was not home. Had she been harmed, he would have never forgiven himself for letting her run away from him tonight.

As it was, he wanted to go after her. He was getting frustrated with her running away from the tough conversations. They needed to talk to one another, and they needed to listen to each other. No matter what happened, he refused to give up on her or their marriage.

Morgan and Jesse met the police officers when they arrived. The officers surveyed the area, and determined that due to the amount of damage, the apartment would require a crime scene investigator. While waiting for CSI to arrive, the neighbors began congregating around, creating a scene.

Morgan tried to keep a low profile but was certain more than one person recognized him.

Twenty minutes later, Morgan and Jesse were talking to the lead investigator when Kyna arrived. She parked as close as she could get and ran toward her apartment. Morgan ran behind her, stopping her before she made it to the building.

"Kyna! You can't go in just yet," Morgan told her.

"Why not? It's my apartment. And how did you get here so fast?" she asked, taking a step away from Morgan.

"Did you forget your security system alerts me also?" Morgan ran his hand over his head. Even now, she was pulling away from him.

Morgan watched Kyna turn her face downward in acknowledgment that she had forgotten. He noticed how she fidgeted with her hands and rocked her body back and forth. He wanted to comfort her, hold her in his arms, but she did not seem to be approachable.

"How much longer do I have to wait?" Kyna asked, pulling her bottom lip between her teeth.

"Until they have completely searched the place. Kyna, be prepared; someone really ransacked your place." Morgan took a step toward her and then noticed her waver. He was there to catch her when her knees buckled beneath her.

One of the police detectives approached them and informed Kyna that she could enter her apartment and look around for anything missing. Morgan stayed right beside her, holding her hand. Even when she tried to pull away, he wouldn't let go.

Morgan helped Kyna step over her tossed furniture and broken items. Suddenly, she stiffened and turned to him and whispered, "My safe." The safe was in the back of her closet, hidden under her dirty clothes hamper. She breathed a sigh of relief when they found the safe untouched. She entered her code and found everything in its place.

Kyna was an emotional wreck and could no longer hold her tears. Morgan continued to hold her close. He felt she needed to feed off of his strength. She just stood there, crying but not saying anything.

"Kyna, baby? You can't stay here tonight," Morgan said.

"I can go to Karmyn's for the night," she responded, with no emotion.

"No! You will come home and stay with me." Morgan asserted his tone to make sure she understood that was final. Unfortunately, she disagreed with him.

"I can't."

Morgan was tired of hearing her say that. She said it earlier in the restaurant and then again at the waterfront. He decided not to mention that, but instead, reminded her of the condo they owned. "Kyna, you know our condo is big enough for both of us to stay and not run to each other. Let me take care of the apartment, then we can leave."

Kyna reluctantly agreed, and after she checked every room for missing items and gathered a few of her belongings, Morgan led her back to his vehicle. She didn't say a word and sat in the car, looking miserable. He wanted desperately to know what she was thinking. But she was intent on being angry.

Morgan and Jesse talked to the police, and Kyna sat patiently, waiting. He didn't want to believe it, but maybe this was God's way of pushing them together. Morgan smirked, thinking, *Only God.* He had a way of making things happen when you didn't want them to.

Morgan approached the car and slid into the driver's seat. Jesse followed behind them, driving Kyna's car. The tension in the car was as thick as fog. He wasn't going to push her into talking. Not yet, anyway.

Only 10 minutes into the drive, Kyna spoke so low, Morgan barely heard her. "I guess you're happy now."

"What do you mean?" Morgan could read between the lines, but he anxiously wanted her to talk to him.

"You have been trying to get me to move into that condo since we got married." She didn't look at him, instead kept her face and body turned toward the window.

"If I didn't know better, I might think you are over there believing I had something to do with the break-in," he said through gritted teeth. Morgan was getting angry, but he promised himself he would not get mad at her. He had been more than patient with her. But insinuating he may have had something to do with this was a low blow.

"I never said that. But it is convenient, isn't it?"

Morgan was going to respond but thought better of it. At least three times during the drive, Kyna had received a text message that she didn't respond to. Morgan couldn't help but wonder who would be texting her at this time of night. Instead of questioning her actions, he let it go. The fight wasn't worth it.

He was trying to be understanding of her feelings. Yes, her home was violated, but her attitude toward him was getting on his last nerve. They drove in complete silence the rest of the way to the condo. Morgan parked in the attached garage and waited for Jesse to park in the driveway behind him. Kyna stayed in the car while Morgan spoke to Jesse about the security of her apartment. He then opened her door and assisted her from the vehicle.

Kyna stood in the middle of the kitchen, looking around. Morgan realized she had never been to the condo, opting to stay in her apartment.

"This is your home. Get comfortable. Walk around and check the place out."

He left her standing there and retreated to his office—anger steeping and causing him to shut down and not wanting to engage with her. Morgan was still trying to calm down from her accusation about his involvement with her apartment. She could be mad at him, accuse him of being jealous, even believe he spent too much money; but, he would not accept her believing he would do such an atrocious act like vandalize her home.

He paced the confines of his office until Jesse entered.

"Whoever did this appears to be a couple of kids. There were three of them; they wore hoodies and baseball caps. The cameras never got a good look at them. They were in and out in under a minute. Doesn't appear that they stole anything," Jesse reported.

"Have a cleaning crew in there first thing in the morning."

"Yes, sir." Jesse turned on his heels and left Morgan to continue brooding.

Morgan remained in his office a few minutes longer. Taking a deep breath, he went in search of Kyna. He noticed she had turned off the lights on the first level, which he took to mean that she went to bed. Morgan loosened his tie and climbed the stairs preparing for the inevitable.

When he entered his bedroom, he noticed Kyna was not there. Her sleeping in another room under the same roof was not going to happen. He searched the guestrooms until he found her in the room furthest away. So she thought she would put distance between them.

Morgan opened the door and found her curled up on the bed. He knew she was not asleep because of the sigh she emitted when he opened the door.

"Not in this lifetime, wife. We sleep in the same bed." He angrily stalked to the bed and grabbed her up into his arms.

"Morgan!" she yelped. "Why can't you understand? I don't have the power or the strength to resist you."

He gazed into her eyes and could see the glistening tears streaming across her cheeks. He whispered, "Then stop trying."

Chapter 12

The next morning, Morgan awakened to an empty bed. He was prepared to be angry until he saw the note on the pillow beside him.

GOING TO BREAKFAST WITH MY SISTERS – TELLING THEM EVERYTHING

Morgan decided that he would need to put a plan into action to win his wife back. First, he had to determine what the real problem was. After reflecting on the past few weeks, he realized that part of the problem they were having was his traveling and not being available to her. The other issue that continually popped up was the secrecy of their marriage. That could be handled quickly. Morgan called John and Melissa to have a quick conference.

"What in the world is so important that we had to have a conference call early on a Saturday morning?" John grumbled.

Morgan knew that John was probably still asleep, but that didn't matter. He needed to get this out in the open, and he had to start with his business partners and siblings. He would tell Grant about his marriage later.

"Oh John, wake up for this. It's a doozy. Go ahead, brother," Melissa retorted.

"John, what Melissa is apparently still upset about is not knowing I got married a few months ago."

A thump was heard, and it sounded like John dropped the phone before coming back on the line, "I'm sorry, it sounded like you said you got married. Months ago."

"Yep, that's exactly what he said," Melissa interrupted.

"Why wouldn't you tell us, and who is this mystery woman?" John asked, now fully awake and livid.

"John, you know her and her sisters." Melissa was intent on making this difficult for Morgan. He hadn't expected it to be easy, but he didn't need her added fuel to the fire. "Go ahead, big brother, tell him," Melissa added.

"Why don't you tell him? Since you keep interrupting," Morgan was annoyed at Melissa stepping in. She was being annoying on purpose.

"This is your story. You tell it," she responded sweetly.

"My wife is..."

Melissa interrupted again, "Kyna Hammond, the youngest sister to Kaleigh Hammond."

There was a short silent pause before John yelled, "Morgan, seriously? How could you?"

Morgan felt he was being chastised by his parents. This conversation would go no better than the one he would have to have with them. He hoped Kyna was faring better with her sisters than he was with his siblings.

"It's not like we planned it. It just sorta happened," Morgan replied. "We met, we had a really long first date, and we married. When you know, you know."

John released a slow, long breath, "Wait until Grant finds out. He is going to blow a gasket. He has been trying to date Kaleigh for months."

"But John, what about the middle-eastern investors?" Melissa asked. "You know, the ones that were hesitant that none of us were married in the first place. They are going to feel lied to once this comes out."

"Morgan, you are not going public with this, are you? Please say not until the deal is done." John changed his tone back to business.

"I have to. Kyna and I have been having some issues, and one of them is around this secrecy."

That was the real purpose of this meeting. The investors had concerns about doing business with unmarried people—something to do with their religious beliefs. However, after a thorough presentation, no one could deny the deal would be advantageous to everyone.

"Oh God, that was a $900 million deal," John cried.

"Stop it!" Morgan barked. "I'll take care of things. I have a call scheduled with the group this morning."

Everyone was silent for a few minutes, each in their own thoughts. Morgan had to smooth things over with the investors or never hear the end of this from his brother. John finally broke the awkwardness.

"Are you going to tell Mom and Dad before you tell the world?" Melissa asked.

"I have to. Can you imagine what would happen to me if I didn't?"

"World war three," the siblings said in unison.

*****

Kyna had cried most of the night. Last night was the first time they slept together and had not touched one another. It was all her fault, and she couldn't be mad at Morgan. She was the one creating the distance between them. Now she was at breakfast having to tell her sisters what should have never been a secret to begin with.

She was the first to arrive and was glad that the restaurant was empty. The Double Egg was a small place with the best breakfast options. The owner/chef always walked around, greeting patrons. The servers would ask for everyone's name at the table and always seemed to remember each person. They spoke to you like you were old friends.

Kyna ordered toast and coffee for everyone before they arrived. Karleigh and Karmyn walked in together before the server returned with their coffee.

"Where is Poe?" Kyna asked.

"She's not responding to calls or texts. I think she just needs time to process everything." Karmyn sat in the chair next to Kyna. Karleigh sat across from her.

Kyna understood Poe needing to be alone, but it was unusual for her. She was the sister that wanted and needed to be surrounded by family in confusing times. The past year, Poe had been dealing with health issues. That may be why she seemed to be withdrawn at times.

"It's okay. We will fill her in later," Kyna said.

After ordering their breakfast, Karleigh jumped right in. "Karmyn says you have some big news to tell us."

Kyna started twisting her hands around her napkin. She couldn't make direct eye contact with Karleigh, or she would start crying again. Instead, she stared at the salt shaker on the table in front of her. "First, don't be mad. We had our reasons."

"Who is *we*?" Karleigh asked.

"Shhh, let her tell you," Karmyn answered. Grabbing Kyna's hand and giving it a light squeeze for support. "Go ahead, sister."

Kyna took a deep breath, then released it. She gathered all the strength she could and sat straight up. Looked her sister directly in the eyes and told her story. "A few months ago, I met a handsome, wonderful man while celebrating with friends. A week later, we got married."

Karleigh exploded. "Sister, tell me you didn't?" She looked to Karmyn, who was sitting back, enjoying the scene unfold. "This had better be some kind of joke."

"Oh, it gets better," Karmyn said, taking a sip of her coffee.

Not waiting for Karleigh to calm down, Kyna continued. "I married Morgan Hawkins."

Kyna and Karmyn waited for Karleigh to piece the information together.

"Grant's brother? The billionaire mogul that just bought an entire hotel near the medical center? The same man that hired your sister to help broker the purchase of said hotel. Please tell me this wasn't some type of quid-pro-quo."

"Dang sister, what am I a prostitute? No! I didn't even know about the hotel until after we had decided to get married," Kyna stated.

Karleigh had a way of making her sisters feel bad about a decision they had made. Most of the time, they were terrible decisions. But in this case, she had no way of knowing that yet. And still, she managed to insinuate that Kyna married Morgan as some type of business deal for Kaleigh.

"Sorry, that's not what I meant." Karleigh reached for Kyna's hand. "How did you manage to keep this a secret?"

Kyna went on to tell Karleigh all of the details, including last night's break-in of her apartment.

"Oh wait, that's new to me," Karmyn said. "Someone broke into your apartment? Why didn't you come back to my house?"

Kyna flashed a fake smile at her sister. Just thinking about how Morgan stepped in to take care of her and her apartment. He was really being a knight in shining armor, and all Kyna could do was complain. "Because Morgan was there taking care of everything."

"Like a good husband would do," Karmyn said.

"Sister, I don't know what to do." Kyna pleaded. "My heart trusts him, and I don't believe he would do anything to hurt me, but I can't get over the feeling that maybe I rushed things, and I'm going to be publicly humiliated."

"Well, I'll tell you this much. Marriage is hard. If it were easy, everyone would be married. If you love him like you say you do. Fight. Don't make it easy for any woman to get next to him. Tell the world who you are," Karmyn said, looking despondent.

Kyna wondered if that was the problem with Karmyn's marriage. Maybe she thought she should have fought harder. Karmyn stayed closed-lip about the details surrounding her divorce. No one ever pushed, and she never gave.

"I agree, sister," Karleigh added. "Stop hiding in the shadows, sit down with your husband, talk to him. Communication is key to any good relationship."

Kyna's thoughts were interrupted by her work pager going off.

"Looks like I have to go into the office. I wonder what is going on at the hospital." Kyna returned the pager to her purse and retrieved her wallet.

"Are you going to tell Grant?" Karleigh inquired.

"No, that is for Morgan to tell his family."

"When are you going to tell Mom and Dad?" Karmyn asked.

"We'll see. That is not something I look forward to doing." Kyna tossed a few dollars on the table to cover her portion of the meal and rushed out of the restaurant.

On the drive to the hospital, Kyna had time to reflect. She thought about what her sisters said, how her marriage got to this point and her personal feelings. She realized her anger wasn't really with Morgan; it was with herself. She allowed outside influences to shape how she saw issues in her marriage. Morgan never gave her a reason to doubt him. They had discussed keeping the marriage a secret before ever taking their vows. So why was it a problem now? Because she wanted to be open, she wanted to change the agreement.

Kyna arrived at the hospital to a celebration in her department. The medical director and a few board members were setting up balloon decorations. There was a drink station in the corner. Kyna was confused when she walked further into the ward.

The woman who had caused so much trouble for her sister Poe and Grant was talking to an administrator. Why was she here? And where was Grant? Kyna looked around, attempting to find someone who could answer her questions.

"Nurse Kyna, we are so glad to see you," the medical director said her.

"What is this all about?" Kyna asked.

"We just found out that your grant proposal was awarded the prestigious honor. The hospital couldn't be happier for you and Dr. Hawkins."

Excitement replaced the melancholy feeling she had before arriving. She was bubbling with joy as she let his words set in. The million-dollar research grant was based on the research from her doctoral thesis. Dr. Hawkins had been working on similar research when they decided to join forces and apply for the grant.

"I don't know what to say," Kyna was truly speechless. The application process was brutal. They worked day and night to provide everything the selection committee asked for.

"Don't say anything, just celebrate." The medical director jovially strutted away.

The grant award would bring prestige to the hospital, and it also came with a million-dollar match donation to the hospital. Temporarily, Kyna's problems slipped away as she celebrated with her colleagues.

Her joy was short-lived when Hannah cackled loudly from where she was still talking with a hospital administrator. Dr. Hawkins ex-fiance was continually turning her nose up at the nurses and other hospital staff but smiling and prancing in front of the hospital administrators.

Kyna was talking with another nurse when her phone began vibrating in her pocket. She took a look at the message and returned the phone to her pocket. The text messages she had been receiving from Bruce were becoming a pain in the rear.

He kept asking her out to dinner and assuming that she needed a real meal, whatever that meant. She tried, unsuccessfully, to decline his invitation, but he kept pressing it. She couldn't take it anymore and blocked his new number.

Kyna was sure that wouldn't stop him. Unfortunately, this would be another thorn she would have to deal with.

The party was going well, and after Dr. Hawkins arrived, the medical director gave a short speech congratulating the two. Along with the speech, the entire staff was given a pay increase. That caused a loud celebration among everyone.

Kyna escaped the party as quickly as she could. Hannah was making the party unbearable, and Kyna had no more fakeness left in her body. Grant had finally put Hannah in her place. Kyna was liable to place her fist solidly into the woman's face if she approached her one more time with her elitist attitude.

The drive back to the condo was taking longer than usual. Kyna was not looking forward to facing Morgan. They needed to talk, but that was easier said than done. She was still struggling with what to do. Her sisters had been quite vocal about what she should do. Taking their advice was probably in her best interest, but she didn't know how to approach it.

Why was it so hard to do the right thing? While she drove around the city, she ended up at the Riverwalk. Kyna decided to take a walk and think. Her thinking session turned into a one-sided conversation with God.

She first prayed for discernment before verbally speaking the entire situation aloud. Kyna didn't care that people were staring at her as she seemed to talk to herself. After laying out the situation, she thought about the areas that were of her own volition.

Next, she prayed to God for direction. Instead of trying to figure out her next steps alone, she leaned on the everlasting

Lord. Then, Kyna sat on a bench facing the water and just relaxed. She closed her eyes and listened. The birds seemed to chirp louder, and the sounds of the waves hitting the side wall crashed harder. But, the voices of people walking by were muted. She only heard the beauty of nature.

Then, like a booming voice, Kyna heard the word Now. She opened her eyes and looked around. The voice sounded so close, but there was no one nearby. Kyna had an idea, like a click in her brain. Suddenly, she no longer felt unsure of what to do. A peace or calm came over her. She reached for her cell phone, which was at the bottom of her purse. She eagerly typed out a text message to Morgan.

MEET ME AT THE PLACE WE FELL IN LOVE.

She didn't have to wait long. Morgan walked with an effortless swagger that Kyna loved. His long strides and intense eyes staring into her soul made her fall in love with him all over again. Love at first sight was real, and she no longer questioned why she said yes to his marriage proposal.

He was wearing a blue button–up shirt, neatly tucked into his well–fitting jeans. Kyna also noticed he was wearing his wedding band. That simple act caused her stomach to roil over, and she fixated on what it could mean. Was he telling the world they were married? She took a moment to catch her breath.

"I'm glad you could meet with me so quickly," Kyna told him.

"You are my wife. I would do anything for you." Morgan took the seat next to her.

"Anything? If you mean that, I think this will be easier than I thought," Kyna smiled.

"And why is that?" Morgan asked, not giving her an inch.

"Morgan, I love you so very much. I want us to work on having a real marriage and not one hidden in the shadows of reality. I want our families to know about us. I want them to see us married and in love."

Kyna felt Morgan's hand gently grasp hers. He slightly squeezed it for reassurance. Then she felt him pushing her wedding ring on her finger. The action caused the dam of tears to break, and she began sobbing uncontrollably. She tried to talk, but Morgan embraced her tightly to his chest and just held her.

"Shhh, baby. No words are needed." He used his thumb to wipe away the tears that trailed her cheeks.

They stayed in this position for several minutes. She enjoyed the comfort of his arms, and he seemed to not want to let her go. Eventually, they allowed a little space between them, but not much. Morgan stared down into her tear-stained face and kissed her forehead, then her temples on each side. With each kiss, he recited his wedding vows, and by the time he made it to her lips, he said, "nothing but death could keep me from you."

Kyna laughed at the line from her favorite movie, "The Color Purple." Morgan joined in on the laughter, and together they felt their bond becoming stronger.

Chapter 13

The next morning Kyna and Morgan were greeted by the morning news headlining their marriage. They had no idea who leaked the information, but the article included a photo from their time at Dollywood and a picture of them on the riverfront from the previous day.

Bridget had to be behind this. She was the only person, other than Jesse, who knew they had been to Dollywood. Knowing that this information was now public, they each checked their cell phones and emails. There were several messages from all of their siblings. The couple looked at one another and laughed. It was going to be an interesting day.

A pounding on the door alerted Morgan that his brother had arrived. John sent a text message a few minutes before Morgan had awakened. Kyna stayed in the bedroom to respond to her many messages from her sisters. If they had to face the firing squad, at least they would do it together.

Kyna was hitting send on the first text message to her sisters when she received a call from Kevin and Kyra Hammond, her parents.

"What is the meaning of this?" Her father growled. Before Kyna answered, she heard her mother in the background saying, "Is it true?"

"Dad, what's true is that I am married to a wonderful man." Kyna placed her phone on speaker so she could talk with her parents and get dressed. She was sure John would not be the only person to stop by. She entered the great room when her father asked the next question.

"What about this article in the paper? They are saying you are pregnant."

"Pregnant?" Kyna shouted. That caught the attention of Morgan and John. "I am not pregnant."

John gave Morgan a questioning look; which Morgan returned with a hit upside the back of his head. Like Kyna predicted, there was another knock at the door. This time it was Grant. He gave Kyna a slight nod upon entering and continued to the kitchen where his brothers were.

Her father was saying something when chaos broke out in the kitchen. Kyna didn't know if the brothers were fighting or what, but she quickly ended the call with her parents after inviting them to dinner that evening.

She raced into the kitchen to find chairs knocked over and Grant on the floor with Morgan in a headlock. "What is going on in here?" Kyna folded her arms across her chest.

"They are big kids, don't mind them," John laughed as he tried to get between the two of them.

Kyna put her hands on her hips in a dramatic fashion to show her disdain. The brothers finally got to their feet, with Morgan giving Grant a final shove in the back. They straightened the chairs and sat silently at the table.

"Explain," Kyna gritted out while tapping her foot against the floor.

"Grant thinks our marriage will push Kaleigh away," Morgan threw an apple at Grant, which he caught before it hit his head.

This was a side of Morgan she had never seen. To be honest, she had never seen him in any setting other than with her. She could see Morgan playing with their children one day. The thought settled in her spirit.

"Oh please, Poe will come around. She just needs time to evaluate the situation and realize you are the best man for her. You know she overthinks everything." Kyna gave Grant a reassuring smile.

The brothers settled down long enough for Morgan to call his parents. They had heard the news on the news like everyone else. His parents didn't seem as angry as her father. At least there wasn't any yelling that she could make out from their conversation. Morgan invited his parents to dinner and was sending a private jet for them.

Kyna didn't want to take their parents to a restaurant for dinner. She wanted to prepare a home-cooked meal for her in-laws and her husband. She needed to impress the elder Hawkins and ensure they knew she was a good wife despite her age. The subject of age was sure to come up. There was a 13 year age gap between Morganand Kyna.

The menu Kyna prepared was simple, baked honey glazed chicken leg quarters, with broccolini and a side salad. For dessert, she wanted to surprise her husband with his favorite, banana pudding. It also happened to be her father's favorite dessert. The evening had to be perfect.

Everything was going great in the kitchen until Kyna realized there were no Nilla wafers for the banana pudding. She had to go to the grocery store, and Morgan had been in his office for the last hour. Not wanting to disturb him, Kyna grabbed her car keys, cell phone and made her way out of the house. She drove to the nearest market. They had to have what she needed.

While in the store, she also grabbed a bottle of champagne. As bad luck would have it, she ran into Bruce. Kyna had blocked his calls and text messages for the past few days. She had hoped he was getting the message that she was not interested in him. Unfortunately, it didn't seem that way.

"Well, if it isn't the billionaire's wife." He said "billionaire" like it tasted disgusting in his mouth. Kyna rolled her eyes at his juvenile antics. "You should have told me you preferred rich men. Is that why you haven't returned my calls? I didn't make enough money for you?"

Kyna tried to ignore him. It was useless trying to reason with an idiot. Bruce was clearly pumped up on his own ego to realize he never stood a chance with her. She attempted to walk past him when he reached out and grabbed her arm.

"Let go," she said through clenched teeth. She was seething mad. How dare he put his hands on her. She tried to snatch her arm away when he didn't immediately follow her directive. But he held firm.

"Not until you tell me the truth. When we dated, was I just a joke to you? Were you looking for a big payday? You women are all alike."

He didn't wait for a response from Kyna. When he spoke, she smelled alcohol on his breath. Bruce was clearly intoxicated. There was no one else around in the store, so Kyna lowered her voice when responding.

"I don't know what you are talking about, but if you don't let my arm go, I will scream bloody murder and drop a foot where the pain is unbearable," Kyna said the last statement with a devilish grin that made Bruce immediately let go of her arm and take a step back.

"Making a fool of me, you will pay for this."

Kyna walked away without further response. She thought she should tell Morgan about his threat but dismissed Bruce and his neurotics. If Bruce tried something else, she would definitely let her husband know what was going on.

She made it back home before either set of parents arrived. His parents would probably arrive early, because they were coming straight to the condo from the airport. Her parents would probably be right on time.

Kyna caught Morgan in the kitchen, peeking into the warming dishes.

"Hey you, out of the kitchen." Kyna grabbed a towel from the counter and swatted Morgan with it.

"It smells good in here." Morgan replaced the lid on the dish.

"Your parents will be here soon. I need to finish dessert and change my clothes," she swatted him again when he tried to peer into her bags.

Morgan grabbed the towel, pulling her closer. He then wrapped his arms around her waist, "First, tell me about Bruce?"

Kyna stiffened a little bit and tried to back out of his embrace. "What about him?" she stammered over her words just a little.

"Kyna, someone broke into your apartment two days ago," he released her. "Jesse is always close by, and he saw Bruce talking to you at the store. So don't play coy."

She felt busted but didn't do anything wrong. "You know, at first, I thought it was endearing that you had someone looking out for me when you were away, but now it's annoying. You can call off Jesse. I don't need a babysitter." She twisted out of his arms, and he let her go.

So much for their truce. Kyna was fuming now. How dare he ask her about Bruce. Nothing was going on, but why did his jealousy seem like over-protection and hers seemed psychotic. Maybe it was because whenever he questioned her, she erected a wall of deflection.

Looking back on what just happened, she could have handled it differently. Mostly since she was sure Jesse told Morgan how Bruce grabbed her. Why did she always have to overreact to everything?

She refused to let this minor issue interfere with their evening. A hot shower and fresh clothing should relax her enough to appear normal when her parents and in-laws arrived. Just thinking about the two sets of parents meeting for the first time was causing her some mild anxiety. That anxious feeling was overtaking the anger she felt when she entered the bedroom.

After her shower, Kyna selected a red Armani pantsuit and paired it with some simple slipper flats and modest jewelry, including her wedding ring and diamond stud earrings. She was feeling much better and ready to take on anything that happened next.

Just as she was finishing her hair, the doorbell rang. That anxious feeling returned ten-fold. So maybe she wasn't ready after all. She heard Morgan talking and laughing. His parents must have been the first to arrive. She pasted on a smile and sauntered from the bedroom and into the living room.

She was shocked to see her parents standing with Morgan.

"There's my baby," Kyra Hammond walked over and embraced Kyna in a tight hug.

"Hi, Mom. Dad. So glad you could make it."

"Of course we could make it," Kevin Hammond said, watching Morgan while hugging his youngest daughter. "It's not every day a father finds out his baby girl is married in a newspaper. But we will talk about all of that later."

"Yes, Daddy."

There was an awkward silence, and Kyna wasn't sure what to do next. Morgan stared at her, and her parents looked back and forth between the two of them. Kyna was thankful for her mother speaking first.

"Kyna, show us around. This is a lovely home you have here," Kyra looked around the spacious condo.

"How long have you been living here?" Kevin asked.

Before she could answer the question, the doorbell rang again. They all turned toward the door as Morgan went to answer it. Marilyn and Lawrence Hawkins were a stunning couple. Morgan clearly resembled his mother, but had his father's height. Again Kyna was tongue-tied after the introductions were made.

Morgan jumped in when he realized Kyna wasn't going to say anything, "I'm so glad everyone could make it tonight. It will just be the six of us. My beautiful wife made us a wonderful dinner." He pulled her close to his side. "Shall we make our way to the dining room?"

Morgan gave Kyna a quick squeeze, then led the couples into the dining room. The table was previously set. Kyna was adamant that she did not want any servants in the condo during dinner. After everyone was seated, Morgan and Kyna served their parents and then themselves before sitting to say grace. Kyna closed her eyes and silently prayed for strength to make it through the evening. Amazing how earlier she felt strong enough.

Kyra gave her daughter a wink after the prayer was over. She knew that meant Morgan was getting points in her mother's book. The Hammonds were a spiritual and religious family. Believing in God was non-negotiable in their household. Their parents didn't have a fight from the sisters. They experienced early in life the love of the Lord.

Not much was said during dinner. The conversation stayed very light, only discussing the weather, a little bit about sports, a few questions about working with Grant and accolades for how wonderful the food tasted.

They finished their meals and had moved to the living room for after-dinner drinks. Kyna and Morgan sat together on one end of the large sofa. They held hands and waited for the interrogation. Kyna needed his support more than she thought. Even though they had a little spat before the parents arrived, she knew he would stand by her side.

"Let's please address the elephant in the room," Marilyn Hawkins stated. "One of you should start from the beginning and don't stop talking until we tell you to."

Morgan started with how they met. Kyna only spoke when she needed to fill in the blanks. Both sets of parents remained quiet while they retold their whirlwind one week courtship and wedding.

"It sounds so romantic, but you two didn't really think this through, did you?" Marilyn asked.

"No, we didn't," Morgan answered his mother.

"Today, it was one paper and one sleazy internet site. Tomorrow, it will be more and more until another story or scandal takes your place. Morgan! You know better than this," Marilyn reprimanded him like a little boy.

"Yes, Mom."

"Kyna, he probably has not told you what to expect tomorrow or when you go back to work, has he?"

Kyna looked bewildered and tried to get some type of subliminal support from Morgan. "No, ma'am."

"Well, let me explain. Not only will you be hounded by the press because you were able to marry a billionaire, but they will come after your family."

Kyna heard her mother attempt to stifle her gasp.

"Marilyn, what do you mean by 'come after' my family?" Kevin asked.

Lawrence explained, "The media is going to want to know everything they can about Kyna and her family. Not only that, if they don't like what they hear, they will begin to make things up to sell papers. Your family is about to be turned upside down. And Morgan knows this."

"Morgan, what is he talking about?" Kyna asked her husband. She moved away slightly to see him fully. He hadn't said much, except to keep his head down.

"Several years ago, when I closed my first multi-million dollar deal, I was dating Bridget. She was convinced that I was going to propose to her. She began making plans, and her plans were leaked to the media," he solemnly said.

Kyna wasn't sure how to receive this information. She didn't know that he and Bridget dated. She was under the impression that they knew each other from the circles they were in. Now, knowing that they had a relationship changed a few things for her.

"And that media circus almost drove Melissa to a meltdown. She had been doing her best in the communications department, but being a new graduate and thrust into a position she wasn't ready for caused her too much stress," Marilyn added.

"My sister had to take a sabbatical during that time. We hired an outside company to handle the media." Morgan looked around at the parents before setting his gaze on Kyna.

"That one reporter slept in his car in front of our house. He used some of the best technology to take pictures. Then he made up stories to sell papers. It was horrible," Marilyn continued.

"Why didn't you tell me this?" Kyna lowered her voice to ask.

"I apologize. It was one of the reasons why I wanted to keep everything a secret. We could enjoy ourselves without being harassed until we were ready to announce. I'm sorry, baby."

Morgan tried to reach for Kyna, but she flinched and quickly recovered after seeing her mother's stare. Kyra was perceptive and undoubtedly saw the change in emotion.

"Well, what is your plan for handling the media fallout?" Kevin asked, directing his question to Morgan. Her father wasn't about to let Morgan off the hook. Especially if it meant harm may come to his family. Like Morgan, Kevin was fiercely protective of the women in his life.

"Melissa is on top of things. She only recently found out herself, but she is working with a team of people to minimize any damage. As for your privacy, I have a security team on standby, should you want their services."

The room fell silent again, everyone seeming to be in their own thoughts. Kyna was afraid to move or speak. She was causing her own angst by overthinking items she heard. It didn't appear that anyone was planning to make a move. Kyra, the ultimate hostess, stepped up again for the save.

"Marilyn, Lawrence, it was a pleasure to meet you both. I hope we get to talk again soon." Kyra smoothly ended all thoughts and conversations about the media or security. "I think it is time for us to leave."

"Kyra, it was a pleasure, and your daughter is very lovely. I think with time, we will forgive these two and love them once again." The two mothers laughed. The fathers seemed to be holding back.

Morgan and Kyna escorted their parents to their vehicles and watched them leave. Once out of sight, Kyna left Morgan's side and went straight to their bedroom. She had so much to think about, again. Right when she thought she had everything figured out, her mind runs rampant with what-if scenarios.

*****

Morgan shouldn't be upset with her; he had intentionally not discussed any previous relationships with her. To his defense, Kyna never mentioned her old relationships, except for Bruce Shaw. He was becoming a nuisance. This would be the second time he has made an appearance and harassed Kyna.

Jesse had already reported that the man was single and lived alone. He was living way above his means in an attempt to be someone who he clearly was not. The report Morgan received on Bruce included a credit report that showed he was in significant financial debt. Before turning in for the night, Morgan wanted to check in with Jesse.

The evening seemed uneventful, according to the security team. The Hammond sisters and Hawkin's siblings were safe and sound with no paparazzi in sight. Knowing that would help Morgan rest well for the night.

The bedroom was dark when he entered. Kyna had already gone to bed. He could tell she was still awake by her breathing, but he didn't want to ruffle her feathers any more than they already were. He eased around the room, removing his clothes and finding his pajama bottoms. When he got into bed, he wanted to touch her but instead turned his back to her and fell asleep.

Chapter 14

The next morning, Morgan found Kyna in the kitchen drinking a cup of coffee. She was leaning against the breakfast bar, seemingly dazing into space. He watched her for a few seconds before making his presence known.

She briefly gazed in his direction, then returned to staring straight ahead. He was not going to allow her to act this way. He was frustrated with the hurt little girl routine.

"Good morning."

"Good morning."

She was dressed for the day and looked so beautiful. Her hair was flowing freely around her shoulders. She wore a lip gloss that made her lips appear plump and kissable. His heart expanded, then deflated. He loved her beyond reason, but they had to get over this hump.

"For the record, last night was the last time we go to sleep angry without talking things out first," Morgan firmly said, making his position on the matter clear.

"Is that a command?" she retorted, never looking at him.

"Kyna, don't do this, okay. So, I didn't mention one thing about a past relationship. It's not the end of our marriage."

Placing her coffee cup on the counter, she turned to him. "Morgan, we talked for hours and hours and not once did you mention this. And to make matters worse, it was Bridget, the woman from Gatlinburg. You could have mentioned it then," she paused and stared off.

She was right. Morgan should have said something then, but he didn't think it was a big deal. They both had pasts; Morgan chose to not ask about hers.

"Now, things are beginning to make sense. She is doing this for revenge," Kyna suggested. "She wants you back, doesn't she?"

Morgan didn't want to believe that Bridget was that vindictive, but after the pictures were released from Dollywood, he knew it had to have been a set-up from the beginning, all staged by Bridget.

"I can't change the past." Morgan used his hands to scrubbed down his face and take a deep breath before he continued. "It doesn't matter what she wants. I want you."

She remained silent for several moments. Morgan wasn't sure she would respond at all. He didn't want to push her. Pushing is why they are where they are now. Kyna had to trust him explicitly, or they were doomed.

"Morgan, what's the latest news with my apartment?" Kyna quickly changed subjects.

"I will have Jesse check on it. It has been secured, and a cleaning crew has been scheduled." Morgan walked past her to get his own cup of coffee. She didn't move, making it awkward to step over her long legs.

"I think I'll go to the hospital today. There is a lot of work to be done. Getting the grant award was just the first step. I'll probably spend a lot of time in the lab over the upcoming weeks."

"Kyna, don't put distance between us. Right now is the time to come together. We are stronger together," Morgan pleaded with her.

"Morgan, I have so many different emotions going on inside of me right now. Every time we make two steps forward, somehow we go three steps back."

He noticed she was trying to keep her tears at bay. Her eyes shimmered, showing her turmoil within. "Maybe we need to stop right here and seek counseling. I don't want to go backward anymore." Morgan agreed with her. They did seem to move in this seesaw fashion of up and down.

"Counseling, that sounds good."

Their silence was a mutual agreement to work on their marriage. He would do whatever needed to be done.

"Jesse will be your driver and personal security from now. The media will try to get to you by any means, including every unscrupulous way they can find." Morgan stepped toward Kyna and was grateful she didn't pull away. He kissed her cheek, "Have a good day, baby. I love you."

He left her in the kitchen with her thoughts and sought solace in his office

Morgan was responding to emails when he heard Kyna leave for work a few minutes later. He had been waiting for her to go so he could make a call to Bridget. He didn't want Kyna to hear what he had to say to the woman.

"Bridget Vandersloot," she answered so sweetly. There was no doubt she had caller-ID and knew who was calling.

Morgan dismissed the formalities and got straight to the point. "This is even beneath you. Why would you do this?"

Bridget didn't try to play naive. She wasn't the type of person who would allow someone else to get the credit for something she did, even if it was evil or illegal. "Because she has everything that was supposed to be mine."

Morgan sat at his desk, shaking his head. The woman had lost her marbles if she thought they were ever getting back together. She was shallow and vain, neither of which he saw as redeeming qualities. "I was never going to be yours."

"Why?" Bridget whined. "We were good together. We could have been great."

"Bridget, I was just starting in business, and you were into your career. We would have never worked." Morgan tried to explain for the hundredth time. The same words he said to her almost 10 years ago. They were heading in two different directions.

"You don't know that." He could hear the sadness in her voice. "I hope you are happy." She ended the call without allowing Morgan to say anything further.

Morgan leaned back in his chair, expelling a breath he didn't know he was holding. He prayed that was the end of Bridget and her minion Daneida Bell. Glancing at his watch, he checked Qatar's time before having Raven contact his investors. Morgan was more nervous than he had ever been. These investors were very traditional in their values.

They had concerns about Morgan and John's lack of marital status. They believed single men were flaky in their decision-making. Morgan had convinced the men that would not be the case with The Hawkins Group. Now, they may be proved correct because the investors more than likely heard about him having a wife in the tabloids. Morgan decided the best approach was to be honest.

The line rang right on time. "Morgan, I have Mr. Mustapha on the line," Raven announced.

"Thank you, Raven. Please connect him." Despite still wearing his pajamas, Morgan transformed into business mode and sat straight up in his chair. When he heard the line connect, Morgan began with what he hoped would be a call to address any concerns and keep this deal on track.

"Amir."

"Morgan, I hear that congratulations are in order."

Amir Mustapha was the designated leader of the investment group The Hawkins Group was looking to do business with. This would be the first partnership Morgan would be taking on. It was also the first international project.

"Thank you," Morgan answered.

"I must tell you that my business partners are not pleased."

"I understand. Let me assure you that our business deal is still intact. My marriage was kept a secret to keep the media frenzy out of our lives. My wife is a nurse and has a passion for helping women to have children. Her life's work is in reproductive therapy." Morgan added in Kyna's profession because he knew one of Amir's partners had a wife who was having trouble conceiving.

"I see. Well, we would love to meet your wife. How about we have dinner when my partners and I come to the states to sign the documents?" Amir offered.

"I believe she will enjoy that. I will make the arrangements. We will see you in a few weeks."

Morgan sent Melissa and John an email that the deal was still on and the investors would be in town for a formal dinner in a few weeks. Morgan wanted to make sure the dinner was perfect. He had Raven schedule a dinner reception at the Wilson House.

The Wilson House was a restored mansion once belonging to a union general of the civil war. World-renowned Chef Marcus purchased the house from its previous owners and turned it into a 5-star restaurant.

Morgan had Raven reserve the entire restaurant for the evening. He did not want any interruptions or distractions.

The last thing that Morgan needed to do was to find a credible, reliable marriage counselor. He thought about contacting Kyna's church pastor but decided against it because of how close their family was to the church and the congregation.

Instead, he sent a text message for Raven to find a therapist or counselor in the area. Raven was meticulous and thorough in her research. Morgan trusted her opinion. Within the hour, Raven had sent him three names of counselors. Two were women, and one was male. He settled on Dr. Laverne Stakes after reading through each of the recommendation's background and credentials. She had been in family and marriage Christian counseling for over 20 years. Morgan instructed Raven to schedule the first two appointments.

*****

Kyna was still lost in thought as she arrived at her hospital. Jesse was pulling the sedan up to the staff entrance when a photographer started taking pictures out of nowhere. Jesse quickly maneuvered the vehicle away from a group of other photographers approaching the car. The flashing bulbs were unreal to Kyna, and she immediately ducked her head underneath her hands to hide her face from the cameras.

"Dr. Hawkins, is there another entrance?" Jesse asked

"I don't know," she whispered. Kyna was unable to think straight. She could only see flashing lights.

"Don't worry, I have an idea." Jesse whipped the car out of the parking lot and circled back around the building onto the main road.

Jesse made a call, and within a few minutes, he pulled the sedan into the garage at the emergency room entrance. This area was covered to provide patients privacy from media and ambulance-chasing accident lawyers.

"Will it always be this way?" Kyna asked.

"No, there will be something else for them to attach to soon enough. But I would expect to see them around for a few months.

Kyna entered the hospital through the emergency department and absently walked toward the main lobby. She was swiftly turned around by Grant and led toward the cafeteria.

"Kyna, there are reporters all over the lobby area. You need to be discreet." Grant told her.

"How did you know I would enter this way?"

"Jesse called me. I know you have never dealt with this before. I'm here for you if you need anything, Sis."

Kyna had forgotten that she could now publicly accept that Grant was her brother-in-law. She gave him a half-smile at that thought.

Absently, she followed behind Grant to the service elevator behind the cafeteria. They exited on the 3rd floor, where their office and the laboratory were located. Kyna could hear the murmurs from people as they walked past.

Grant guided her into his office and helped her to the small sofa he had. She was still feeling a little numb to everything. She felt Grant press a cold glass into her hands, and instinctively she took a sip of the cool liquid. A full second passed before she started choking, "What is this?"

"A little whiskey. I figured that would bring you out of your zombie-like state." Grant laughed at her.

"Well, it worked. Yuck." She handed the glass back to Grant.

"You can stay here and get yourself together, come down to the lab or go home."

"I can't go home." Kyna blurted it out before thinking that Grant would want to know why. She couldn't tell him Morgan was at home, and they were not speaking, again.

"Why not?" he asked.

"You wouldn't understand. Besides, I can't talk to you about this. He's your brother."

"Oh, I get it." Grant took a seat behind his desk. "Well, let me tell you this. You are now my sister, and just as I do with Melissa, I promise to listen to you and keep whatever we discuss between us." He paused, "I'm here for you, just like a big brother is supposed to be. And if my brother gets out of hand with you, I will beat him down again."

Kyna laughed, remembering their tussle in her kitchen. She nodded her head in appreciation for the support from Grant. She no longer saw him as the arrogant doctor she first met or the genius he was in his field. He was just Grant, and he was her brother-in-law.

"Thanks, Grant. And before you ask, Poe is still your problem."

Kyna didn't stay in Grant's office. She went into her much smaller office and started checking her emails. There were emails from Karmyn and Karleigh, but none from Poe. There were also a few from Alexis and Chelsea and one from Mario. They all said the same thing; asking how she was doing with the news of her marriage out.

Chelsea felt slighted because Kyna had not confided in her. Mario simply said congratulations. Later, she noticed an email from Morgan. After opening it, the message asked if she would be available that afternoon to meet with the counselor.

Instead of responding, Kyna dropped her head to her desk and cried. After the tears stopped falling, she prayed. What she wanted was confirmation that she had made the right decision. She needed a sign, a miracle, or a wonder. Kyna heard a movement and opened her eyes to see Jesse standing in front of her, offering her a handkerchief.

"Thank you, Jesse. I'm sorry, I'm such a mess." Kyna used the handkerchief to wipe her tears that seem to keep flowing.

"Nonsense Dr. Hawkins." He took a seat in the chair opposite her desk. "I don't usually give my unsolicited advice, but this is an unusual circumstance."

Kyna eyed him suspiciously before he continued.

"I have been working for Morgan for over eight years. He is extremely cautious when it comes to people he allows into his inner circle. Any woman he dated, he always held at arm's length, and that included Bridget Vandersloot. He has always been touted as America's billionaire bachelor, but none of that ever fazed him one way or another. Until you."

"Me? Why me?" she asked.

"Because you give him purpose. If I can be blunt, Morgan loves you beyond measure. He is not nearly as rough around the edges as he has been. He actually hired an assistant for Ms. Raven. I think that is because of you. You are good for him, Dr. Hawkins. Marriage is work. If it weren't challenging, would it be worth it in the end?" Jesse stood, adjusted his suit jacket and left her office.

Kyna sat at her desk with a bewildered look. Jesse, her driver and protector, never said more than "good morning" and good evening,"" sat there and lectured her. He said everything she needed to hear. If she really thought about things, she was more to blame for how she felt than Morgan. They both knew the deal going into this marriage. Yet, she was here again, rationalizing issues she already had answers to.

For the first time in a few weeks, Kyna smiled a genuine smile of happiness. She needed to talk to her husband. And they would talk until everything was in a better place than before, and they would continue to talk until they were both in agreement on their expectations and their future.

Kyna started responding to emails, first letting Morgan know she wanted to talk with him before they moved forward with counseling. The next few emails were to her friends, apologizing for the secrecy and promising to meet them for drinks and tell them everything.

After she sent the last email, Kyna grabbed her lab coat and marched into the research lab with a renewed sense of happiness.

Later, Kyna met her sisters during lunch at the bridal boutique for the final dress fitting. Karleigh's wedding was quickly approaching. So much needed to be done, and still no word from Poe. She hoped her sister was getting the rest she deserved.

Karmyn waved Kyna over when she entered the door. Her sister appeared to be on her third or fourth glass of champagne, courtesy of the bridal boutique. The attendant found Kyna's dress and had her try it on for the seamstress. There didn't need to be many alterations for her gown.

Kyna had dressed and met Karmyn in the suite when Karleigh and Poe walked in. Seeing her sister looking refreshed was a beautiful sight. During the dress fitting, they talked about everything that had happened over the past few weeks, but no one brought up Kyna's new status, Grant or the research award Kyna received. It seemed Poe didn't know that Kyna had married.

"Sooo, Kyna. I saw you on television with Grant receiving some kind of award. You looked good, girl. And, when did you become a doctor?" Poe asked.

For a few seconds, no one said anything. It felt like the air was sucked from the room. The sisters kept looking at one another.

"Yeah, I wanted to tell you with everyone else. I've been so distant over the last few years because I was in school. No one knew," Kyna took a sip of her mimosa.

"So, you really are a doctor?" Poe asked, shocked. "I thought the news just got it wrong."

"I have a doctorate degree in nursing and three master's degrees," Kyna proudly said. "Every time I finished one degree, something awesome was happening in one of your lives." She turned to each of her sisters. "I didn't want to overshadow that. So. I kept it to myself."

"Are you addicted to college degrees or something?" Poe asked in jest.

"She is just an overachiever. Not good enough being the baby of the family, but she had to go and become a doctor," Karleigh teased her.

There was another awkward silence. Poe seemed confused again. Kyna could tell she didn't know what was going on. Her sisters were being distant and not bubbly like they had been just minutes earlier.

"Tell me. Whatever it is, just tell me," Poe demanded.

All eyes turned to Kyna. "I have other news. I didn't want to tell you in a message."

"Spit it out for heaven's sake," Poe demanded.

"I got married a few months ago," Kyna shyly ducked her head.

Poe jumped up, knocking over a small table with a bottle of champagne. "You did what? Why didn't you tell us?"

Kyna retold the story of her whirlwind romance and the issues they were trying to work through.

"You keep saying "him" and "my husband." Who is he?" Poe asked.

Karleigh grabbed the second bottle of champagne, and Karmyn stood up, ready to step in.

"Morgan Hawkins. I didn't want to say anything because mentioning Grant's name around you was fragile," Kyna whispered.

A full minute passed before Poe started hysterically laughing. The other sisters looked at each other and weren't sure if they should laugh or call a psychiatrist.

"You snagged a multi-billionaire that I happen to be working for and whose brother is pursuing me all in one week." Poe shook her head in disbelief. "We need another bottle of champagne."

The sisters hadn't laughed like that in quite a while. Enjoying one another's company was long overdue.

After spending time with her sisters, Kyna returned to the hospital to work a few more hours in the lab. She stretched and yawned, knowing it was time to shut down for the day. Placing her lab jacket on the hook in her office, she grabbed her purse and cell phone from her bottom desk drawer, then sent a text to Jesse, letting him know to meet her in the emergency room garage.

Once settled in the car, she informed Jesse of her plans. "Jesse, I'm meeting my friends at the Vault for drinks."

"Yes, Dr. Hawkins."

He nodded to her in the rearview mirror. Aside from Morgan, Jesse was the only person to call her "doctor." She didn't get her doctorate for the accolades, but for the knowledge. She had a thirst for learning that couldn't be quenched until she reached the top. Even now, she is still learning with her research.

"You know, you can call me Kyna. I feel like you are family, and you shouldn't be so formal." Kyna had started thinking of Jesse as another member of the family. He was always there, looking out for Morgan and herself. She thought of him more of a big brother than a bodyguard. Sure, he was big and brawny, clean-shaven head and a crazy long goatee. But he was gentle and calm; a quiet storm.

"Will your husband understand the informality? I will continue to address you as Dr. Hawkins."

"If you insist." Kyna shrugged her shoulders in defeat and returned to the messages on her phone.

The short drive to the Vault was done in silence. When the sedan approached the front of the building, Alexis and Chelsea were standing outside, waiting and waving.

"Kyna! Oh my God, I've been waiting to see this ring!" Alexis screamed when Kyna stepped out of the vehicle. Chelsea was less interested in the ring and more into Jesse, staring at him open-jawed.

"I don't wear the ring to work," Kyna showed her bare hand. "By the way, this is Jesse."

He had opened the door for Kyna and remained standing by the car.

"Hi," both women coyly responded. Kyna rolled her eyes and ushered them inside of the bar.

"He is scrumptious," Alexis laughed.

"So, you all rich and stuff now, personal driver and everything. How rich are you?" Chelsea asked.

"Rich enough to pay for drinks tonight," Kyna responded. She was not about to get into any details about her finances with them. Not that it was any of their business, to begin with.

"Sounds good to me," the women laughed.

Kyna repeated the story about her and Morgan to Chelsea since Alexis already knew the details. Chelsea, the drama queen that she was, interrupted every few sentences with questions and random off-the-wall remarks. She inserted her opinion as often as possible. Alexis was close to losing her cool with her friend until she pointed out the one person Kyna did not want to see.

"Don't look now, but here comes Bruce," Alexis whispered.

Kyna stiffened and could feel the hairs on the back of her neck rise as he approached. With Jesse somewhere lurking around, she was sure this would get back to Morgan. He approached their table and took the empty seat without asking if he could. All three ladies rolled their eyes and turned away when he started talking.

"Ladies. Kyna, congratulations again on your marriage."

"Thank you," she answered dryly. Not wanting to give him any indication that they wanted his company.

Bruce leaned in and whispered for only Kyna to hear, "Had I known you were looking for a payday, I would have told you about my wealth. We would have been good together."

Without thought, Kyna lifted her hand and slapped the smug look from his face. She hadn't noticed he raised his hand to return the slap until Jesse appeared, dragging Bruce away from the table.

"Oh my God, what is wrong with him? How could you have ever dated him?" Chelsea asked.

"We didn't date long. Besides, he wasn't like this back then." Kyna had never thought Bruce would be so evil. Sure he was arrogant and conceited, but she never thought he was violent.

Jesse soon returned and asked that they leave. The look in his eyes had Kyna agreeing without argument. She might fuss and fight with Morgan, but not when Jesse had a deadly look in his eyes.

Without hesitation, Kyna told her friends she had to leave. They also looked very concerned. If they were in any danger, Kyna was sure Jesse would have said something. She calmed her nerves long enough to give her friends hugs goodbye.

"We understand," Alexis said.

"Are you still paying for the drinks?" Chelsea asked.

Kyna just laughed at her friends, "Yes, I'll take care of it."

Kyna turned to Jesse and said, "Take care of our tab, please, while I go to the ladies' room."

Jesse gave her a displeasing side-eye but allowed her a clear path to the restroom.

She entered the restroom, thankful that it was empty. Kyna looked at herself in the mirror and suddenly realized that everything about her old life was gone. But a peace she had never felt overtook her, and she knew that all would be right with her world. Using a wet paper towel, she patted her face and then smiled. "This is my new life; bodyguards, drama and all."

Kyna exited the ladies' room and was forcibly yanked in the opposite direction. The assailant wrapped a large bicep around her neck, placing his other hand over her mouth, muffling her screams. The smell of cigarettes and sewage mixed around her. As she was being dragged from the bar into the alley, she heard Bruce's voice.

"So you thought you could embarrass me? You thought you were safe with that muscle head?"

Kyna was trying to keep calm and control her breathing. Getting too excited might expend too much energy. She couldn't believe that Bruce would go this far. Her mind was going in a million different places, but the one thing she remembered was if abducted, never let them take you to the second location.

Instinctively, she started flailing her arms and kicking her feet, making it difficult for Bruce to drag her further. He tightened his grip around her neck, cutting off her intake of oxygen. She felt her body going limp when Bruce reached for the car door. Kyna used the opportunity to fight back. Taking her right foot, she scraped the heel of her stiletto down his shin. He yelled out in agony, spewing hateful curse words.

Kyna was able to turn away from him and out of his grasp. She took two steps before Bruce reached her and slammed her face into the trunk of the car. The bright light and burning sensation across her face was the last thing she saw and felt before complete darkness. Though she couldn't see anything, she felt her body falling but never hitting the ground.

An exploding pain in her head prevented her from opening her eyes. She kept trying, and with each attempt, the pain in her head intensified. Kyna knew this was her demise and cried out for every silly thing she ever complained about. Morgan was the best man, and he would be left with only a memory of her jealousy and delusions.

This isn't how she thought her life would end. Yet, she was in an alley with a psychopath, unable to open her eyes. Then she heard a voice. Kyna thought it to be the voice of angels coming to take her to heaven. The voice was getting closer and louder. She couldn't understand what he was saying, but it didn't sound like how she imagined an angel would sound.

Unexpectedly, she felt someone wiping away her tears, and the tenderness she felt couldn't have been Bruce. She felt safe, and a peace that surpasses all understanding took over her body. Kyna wasn't afraid, and she succumbed to the darkness.

*****

Morgan paced the room, not seeing or hearing those around him. When he was first notified that Kyna had been injured, he immediately felt useless. He was not with her. That weight of responsibility had come down on his head like a cement slab. All she asked for was that he be there. Be present in the marriage and show up when they were together.

It took a tragedy to open his eyes. She needed him in so many ways, and he wasn't there. Even though she was saved by the good Samaritan, Kyna needed Morgan to be there.

Jesse heard her screams when he started looking for her. The old man and Bruce were fighting in the alley while a lifeless Kyna laid on the ground. After hearing what happened, Morgan felt powerless for the first time. This was something he couldn't throw his wealth or influence around to fix.

Morgan had Kyna brought directly to the condo and not taken to the hospital. They needed to keep the media away as long as possible. Grant and another doctor came over to assess her injuries. They reassured Morgan that she had a concussion and some bruising, but she would be fine. Morgan contacted her sisters and parents, who arrived with no blame in their hearts. Kevin Hammond gave Morgan a hug and told him he was a good man, but he didn't feel like one. He couldn't protect her.

For three days, Kyna drifted in and out of consciousness. The hired nurse told everyone she would come around soon. The medication she was given for the pain caused her to be loopy. Grant was easing her off of the medication.

The doorbell jarred Morgan from his thoughts. Who could be ringing his bell? He wasn't expecting anyone else, and security had to notify you of guests before allowing them to enter. Morgan felt Grant's arm resting on his shoulder.

"Don't worry, it's just your parents," Grant calmed him.

The older Hawkins had gone to vacation in France right after their family dinner. He didn't contact them because he didn't want to bother them. Morgan knew his parents would be on the first flight back.

"Who called them?" Morgan asked.

"Does it matter? But it was Melissa," Grant laughed. The inside joke is that Melissa was the tattle-tell of the family.

Melissa had returned to New York. She had been handling the fallout from the secret marriage, and now this. She was very good at her job, and Morgan needed to remind himself that she deserved a raise for all of the hard work she does for the company and the family.

John opened the door and briefly hugged his mother before she rushed to Morgan.

"Morgan, I heard about Kyna. How is she?" Marilyn asked, full of concern.

He hugged his mother and held on a little longer than usual. A mother's love and embrace was a prescription right from God. Morgan needed his mother to help him through his most painful life experience. "Grant says she will be fine. The pain medicine has kept her asleep most of the time."

Marilyn kissed Morgan's cheek then walked over to talk with Kyra and Kevin. Morgan's father stood in front of him, and the two stared at one another. Neither knowing what the other was thinking. His father reached for his shoulder, causing Morgan to slightly slump under the gentle pressure. The pressure felt like the weight of the world on his shoulders. Lawrence guided Morgan into the office and motioned for the other men in the room to follow.

Morgan fell into the leather chair behind his desk. Grant and John sat on the sofa against the far wall leaving the two fathers to sit in the wingback chairs in front of Morgan's desk. Morgan was expecting his disappointment and maybe even some anger from Kevin Hammond. Instead, he received compassion.

"Son, I can't imagine how you feel right now. But your wife needs you to be strong. You can't fall apart right now," his father spoke first.

Not wanting to look at his father or Kevin in the eyes, for fear of seeing that disappointed look, he held his head low before responding. "Dad, what do you think I'm doing? I'm being strong. I'm holding it together when I really want to scream."

"Then do that. Scream, cry, shout, hit something. Heck, I want to. That's my little girl in there," Kevin spoke up.

Morgan dropped his head into his hands. "Then why aren't you mad at me? I knew about Bruce Shaw and his issues before this happened. I even knew he had an irrational obsession with Kyna, and I didn't stop him."

"You didn't know he would be at that bar. And you didn't know he would try to abduct Kyna," Grant said.

"Yeah, bro," John spoke. "Jesse is the best in the business. He was there and didn't know what that guy was going to do. They all thought Bruce was in a car on his way home."

Jesse had told them when he got Bruce out of the bar, the security guard put him in a car service and sent him on his way. When Kyna didn't immediately return from the restroom, Jesse went to look for her. The ladies' room was empty. He was about to call Kyna's cell phone when he heard the commotion come from the back door.

"It was pure luck that the homeless guy was in that alley, and Jesse heard the commotion while looking for her," Morgan stated.

"That wasn't luck. That was God," Lawrence said.

Being a man of faith, Morgan believed that the homeless man had been put there by God. Why else would he have been in *that* alley at *that* time of night? And why did he step in when he could have walked away. Jesse still had not found the good samaritan, but Morgan intended to find him and thank him profusely.

Morgan was sitting in a room with his father, father-in-law, and brothers. He felt the need to be honest and transparent with them. "Sometimes, I feel like it was something I deserved. Me and Kyna have been having problems."

"What kind of problems?" Kevin asked.

"Allowing jealousy and insecurities to come between us." Morgan paused, taking a big gulp before continuing, "We had decided to seek counseling."

"That's good," Kevin said. "I think you two should go to counseling, for your marriage and for this trauma."

The room became quiet, and only the sound of the ticking clock could be heard. For several minutes, each man was in his own thoughts.

"You know, I thought that if I gave her the finest things and took her on trips, provided for her financially and her security, she would want for nothing," Morgan told everyone.

"Foolish. Do you hear this, Lawrence?" Kevin snickered.

"Yeah, I hear it," Lawrence laughed.

Morgan looked to John and Grant. Both brothers were just as confused as he was. What was humorous about the thought he just shared?

"A good woman is not interested in your money or your status. What she wants from you is your time, loyalty, love and commitment," Lawrence explained. "Do you think your mother is with me for the money? Heck, I didn't have any money until well after Melissa was born."

Kevin added, "My wife had a better paying job than me when we met. I was still in school. What she loved about me was my commitment to my education. She knew I would be just as committed to our family."

The two men continued laughing.

"You listening back there, Grant. Kaleigh doesn't need your money. She needs your love and support," Kevin told him.

Again the room went silent.

Chapter 15

The mumbled voices seemed closer now. Unlike before, there wasn't one voice, but two. They seemed to be talking to one another. The first voice sounded strangely like her mother; and the other voice sounded like Marilyn, her mother-in-law. Kyna blinked her eyes open a few times, attempting to focus. She noticed the furniture in the room, realizing she was in her bedroom at the condo. But why were her mothers in her bedroom?

The lights were dim and not the blinding, piercing light like before. Finally, able to open her eyes fully and adjust, she saw her mothers standing near the door.

"Why are you two whispering?" Kyna struggled to say.

Both rushed to Kyna, one to each side of the bed. Because of the bed's size, they were both able to sit by her side without hurting her.

Holding her hand, Kyra asked, "Kyna, sweetheart, how do you feel?"

"Like I was hit over the head with a frying pan. What happened, and why are you here?"

Neither mother said anything right away. That scared Kyna beyond measure. She immediately thought something had happened to Morgan.

"Would someone please talk to me?"

"Of course. You were in an, uh, accident," Marilyn started. "You've been home resting for a few days."

"A few days?" Kyna tried to sit up, but the pain in her head exploded, causing her to return to her prone position. She lifted her hand to her face and first felt the I.V. line and then touched her eye and felt the pain and tenderness.

"Oh God, Bruce. He tried to kill me," Kyna remembered the attack. She had been about to go home when he grabbed her. She had a difficult time understanding why he would do that. They dated briefly years ago. What would make a man go to such lengths?

Kyra pressed a cold compress to her face, "Don't talk. Get some rest. I will tell Morgan that you are awake and talking."

"Wait!" she whispered but felt like she yelled out. "Not yet. I need to talk to both of you."

Kyna told her mother and mother-in-law about the troubles that she and Morgan had been having. She needed their advice. Together the women had been married for over 70 years. Who better to ask about keeping your marriage together than these two.

"Sounds like the two of you need to better communicate your expectations," Marilyn responded.

"I agree," Kyra responded. "I have listened to my son-in-law for the past few days. I have watched him take care of you and us. He loves you; that is clear. But you both need to talk about what you expect in your marriage."

"Marriage doesn't guarantee you will be together forever. It takes work and lots of it. But to make it for over 40 years, it takes love, respect, trust, understanding, friendship and faith," Marilyn said.

"Amen to that," Kyra agreed with Marilyn. "You both need to talk to someone, a counselor or therapist."

Kyna nodded her head softly. She knew they were absolutely right. Many of her issues with Morgan and their marriage were due to a lack of trust and understanding. Those were things that they could work on over time, with a little help.

"I love both of you," Kyna managed a smile.

Both mothers left the room to tell everyone she was awake. Kyna managed to roll on her side without much pain. She laid with her back to the door and waited for Morgan. She had so much to say.

Kyna wanted Morgan to know how much she loved him and how she was scared to be the billionaire's wife, but she was up for the challenge. He needed to know that she would work on the green-eyed monster of jealousy and learn to trust more.

The door creaked open and then closed. Kyna inhaled Morgan's masculine scent right away. She always loved the cologne he wore. It made him seem rugged and rough. He walked around the bed to meet her eye to eye. For several seconds they just stared at one another. He sat on the edge of the bed, never breaking the connection. This was how they were, intense and determined about everything.

"Baby, I was so scared when I got that call from Jesse. And when he brought you here, you seemed so fragile." Morgan finally let the tears go. Kyna grabbed his hand and gently pulled him into the bed beside her. "I almost lost you."

She allowed him to cry. No words were needed. "Morgan, I love you. I can see the guilt on your face. Let it go." Kyna started singing "Let It Go" from the movie "Frozen," and they both started laughing. "Ow! It hurts to laugh."

"Then, don't. Please," he pleaded with her. "I hate seeing you in pain. Grant promised me you would be fine." Morgan viewed her up and down as if making sure she was still in one piece.

"I guess he is responsible for this IV bag and the good drugs. Wait a minute, you had a obstetrician look at me? Why am I not at the hospital?" She was joking about Grant being the doctor to examine her. But why wasn't she in the hospital?

"Grant brought Dr. Hawthorne over the first day. A nurse has been here every day since to tend to you. As far as going to a hospital, we needed to have control of the narrative. The media doesn't know the details of what happened. Melissa has been working non-stop. She released the story how we wanted it told. Bruce Shaw is in jail, and we wanted our story out before he had an opportunity to twist his version."

Kyna imagined what the media would have reported if they had nothing but her name. She was glad to have a family like she did. Melissa was the best in the public relations business, or at least that is what she was told. She hadn't had a lot of time to spend with her sister-in-law.

They stayed in silence for such a long time. Kyna thought Morgan had fallen asleep.

"Morgan," she whispered. He moaned, and she continued. "I want to talk about us."

He gently turned over to come face to face with her. He went to raise his hand, and she flinched. Her face was very tender to the touch. Instead, he rubbed her back in a soothing and comforting cadence.

"We don't have to do that right now. We will talk very soon. Right now, I'm sure your sisters want to see you."

"They're here?" she asked.

"Everyone is here. Except for Melissa, she had to return to New York. Raven arrived this morning, and your friends have called every day. These florals started arriving soon after we released the story."

Kyna glanced around the room and really took in the sight of the many floral arrangements she hadn't noticed before. They were beautiful, and the love from others caused her to begin crying.

"Hey, what are those tears for?" Morgan took a tissue from the nightstand and wiped her tears. He then kissed her cheek and gently kissed the bruise around her eye.

"I don't know, just emotional, I guess."

Morgan sat with her for a few minutes longer before leaving to get her sisters. The amount of love she felt from family and friends was more than she expected. Kyna tried again to sit upright with a little more success this time. When Karmyn entered the room, she rushed over to adjust the pillows behind her back.

"Sister, please be careful." Karmyn gushed.

"I'm fine," she replied.

"We have been so worried about you. Morgan wouldn't let us in to see you, only the doctor, the nurse and your mothers. He can be a bully."

"But he's my bully," Kyna smiled. "How bad do I look? I noticed Morgan removed the mirror from the dresser."

Karleigh used her hand to gently caress her face then smooth strands of hair down. "You look beautiful."

"Except for that black eye, you look fine," Poe added.

Karleigh and Karmyn both turned an evil eye on their sister.

"What? It's the truth. She doesn't need you two coddling her. That's what her mothers are for." Poe walked to the opposite side of the bed and sat down. "Your eye and cheek are bruised and swollen."

"Thank God for the guy in the alley," Karleigh said, still rubbing Kyna's wayward strands of hair.

Karmyn told Kyna about the good samaritan and how he and Jesse detained Bruce until the police arrived. Kyna didn't remember anything after being dragged outside of the building. To find out that she was slammed into the car and a stranger had saved her was overwhelming.

"You know, Morgan has been blaming himself. He thinks that there was something he could have done," Karmyn continued.

"We shouldn't have kept everything a secret. This would have never happened." Kyna tried to convince herself.

"We all know that isn't true. No one is to blame but Bruce," Karleigh told her.

"And I hope he goes away for a long time," Poe added.

Kyna continued to talk with her sisters until lunch was prepared. Not having anything to do, the mothers decided to show off their culinary skills and prepare a feast for everyone. Wanting to feel normal, Kyna insisted she join the family in the dining room. With some assistance, Morgan helped her to dress and escorted her into the main living space.

*****

Kyna's recovery was coming along nicely. In the past few weeks, she had begun trauma therapy and together, she and Morgan had begun marriage counseling. They both realized their parents had been right. Communication wasn't the only problem, but communicating expectations was where they lacked, along with a host of other reasons that were now being discovered.

Morgan wanted to surprise Kyna with a mini-vacation. She deserved a break to get away from the laboratory, and they needed time to be alone with one another.

Their dinner with his new business associates had gone well. Mr. Mustapha had been impressed with Kyna and her knowledge of their religion and customs. Due to Mr. Mustapha's and his associate's religious beliefs, the group rarely worked with businessmen who were not married. After meeting Kyna and hearing about her attack, the group understood why Morgan and Kyna had decided to keep their marriage a secret.

During dinner, Mr. El-Hassan and his wife asked so many questions about her research that Kyna joked about billing them for the consultation. They would have happily paid any amount if it helped them to get pregnant. Morgan had impressed the group, and after dinner, they all signed the contracts without hesitation.

Kyna had returned to work in the lab and didn't balk at the idea of having constant security nearby. She quickly found out what it was like to have paparazzi following her every step.

Bruce had taken a plea deal, which was equivalent to a slap on the wrist. Morgan didn't feel bad for the guy at all. He lost his job and already had financial issues. Bruce deserved everything he got.

Morgan walked into the hospital, causing a minor ruckus among the staff. Nurses and patients recognized him from the tabloids and papers. He used the service elevator like always to get to the lab.

For several minutes, he watched his wife working. Going back and forth from looking through a microscope to a notebook where she was taking notes. He marveled at the realization that this was his life, and he had almost lost it.

Morgan no longer took for granted the love that he and his wife shared.

Kyna abruptly looked up from her notes and turned around to find Morgan staring at her. Her smile always melted his heart. He entered the laboratory, and without losing eye contact with her, he approached and planted the most passionate kiss upon her lips.

"I have a surprise for you," he said, still gazing into lovestruck eyes.

"You are a surprise. Let me finish up here. I'll meet you in my office."

"Five minutes or I'm coming back," he promised.

She arrived in less than five minutes and was greeted again with another kiss. "Tell my brother you deserve a bigger office." Waving his arm around, "this is half the size of his."

"Yeah, well, he is a doctor, and I am a nurse."

"You are a doctor, too. Just because yours isn't M.D. doesn't make you less of a doctor." He kissed her hands then helped her into her jacket.

"Where is my surprise?" Kyna asked, trying to stifle a giggle.

"We are going on a trip," Morgan casually announced.

"I can't leave, my sister's wedding is next weekend. We still have work to do."

Morgan was well aware of the amount of work that needed to be done for the wedding. Somehow Kyna and her sisters had roped Morgan and John into making crafts for centerpieces. After several bottles of glitter "accidentally" spilling on the floor, the men, including Simon and Nick, were kicked out.

After seeing first-hand what went into having a wedding, Morgan was thankful that he and Kyna didn't one. But, if her grandmother had her way, there would be a wedding taking place. Still, there would be no huge fanfare to the likes of Karleigh and Simon.

"I talked to Karleigh and Simon. As a wedding gift, I hired a wedding planner to take care of all of the work there is left to do. She told me to tell you to enjoy yourself."

"Where are we going?" Kyna asked.

"I believe we need some fun in the sun. How does a few days on the beach sound? I rented a private villa on Amelia Island."

Kyna jumped into his arms and planted kisses all along his face. To keep her this happy was his only mission in life.

"Eww, you two. Not in the office. This is a place of business," Grant joked as he entered Kyna's office.

"Can't you get Dr. Hawkins a bigger office?" Morgan sternly asked his brother.

"I offered her another office. She turned it down." Grant gave his sister-in-law a wink.

"It's upstairs. I'm not going to be running up and down the stairs." Kyna started shaking her head.

"You heard her, find her an office on this floor, or give her yours," Morgan demanded.

"Morgan, you can't bully me in my hospital," Grant laughed. "I heard you are taking some time off, so enjoy. I will see you at the wedding when you return." Grant kept laughing as he left the office.

Kyna placed her hands on her hips and tried to look upset that Grant knew about their trip before she did. "How does he know we are going away?"

"I had to tell him to see if you could leave before I made arrangements. He told me you guys are in a lull, so I jumped on the opportunity," Morgan told her, while escorting her from the office and down the hall.

"You are the best." Kyna gave her husband a huge smile.

*****

Karleigh and Simon's wedding was perfect. The couple had left their reception an hour before the DJ made the announcement for the last song.

When Kyna heard the song, her head popped up, and she searched for Morgan, who was already making his way in her direction. Watching her husband stalk toward her always made her heart flutter.

"I think they are playing our song, Mrs. Hawkins."

"I believe so. Shall we dance?"

She placed her hand in his, together, they walked to the dance floor. Morgan held her close, and they swayed in time with the beats of the music.

Kyna placed her head on Morgan's shoulder and allowed him to lead her across the dance floor. "You know, your mom gave me some of the best advice."

"And what was that?" Morgan asked after he dipped her in time with the music.

"She said to read First Corinthians, chapter 13, verse 4-8. She told me to replace the word love with your name. If the description fits, then our marriage was worth fighting for. I'm so glad I fought for us."

"Do you remember the verse?"

"I will never forget it. Morgan is patient, Morgan is kind, Morgan does not envy or boast. Morgan is not proud, rude, self-seeking or easily angered. Morgan keeps no record of wrongs and does not delight in evil. Morgan rejoices with the truth. Morgan always protects, always trusts, always hopes and always perseveres. Morgan never fails, just like our love."

Morgan stared down into her face and almost teared up at her declaration of love. They had stopped dancing and just lovingly gazed at one another. There was nothing better than the woman he held in his arms. He would go to his grave, thanking God for this beautiful soul.

ABOUT THE AUTHOR

Award-winning Christian Fiction/Romance author Lisa Washington is a Detroit native and currently residing in Georgia with her family. Washington earned her bachelor's degree in public relations from Wayne State University in Detroit, MI and a master's degree in business administration from Averett University in Danville, VA. It wasn't until she suffered from the stresses of a Ph.D, program that she decided, if she had to write 75-page papers, they would be something she truly enjoyed writing.

Two years later, Washington was accepted into the Master of Fine Arts program for creative writing at Butler University in Indianapolis, IN. She applied with a terrible first draft of her first published novel, "When You Least Expect It." Washington completed her program in 2016. After two years of peer reviews and a year of learning how to self-publish her novel, she went on to win the 2018 African American Literary Award Show, Best Christian Fiction Award for "When You Least Expect It."

Washington also served several years in the US Navy before attending college. Washington credits having a strong faith in God and trusting He had a plan for her life. Her faith is also what drives her to write Christian fiction and romance. She is often quoted saying, "If it were not for God, I don't know where I would be today."

Lisa Washington and her husband are the co-founders of The Washington Way LLC, which includes Washington Way Financial, Washington Way Publishing, Washington Way Travel, and Ms. Lisa Weddings.

ALSO BY LISA WASHINGTON

THE FAITH SERIES

When You Least Expect It

More Than You Know

Love Lifted Me

MY SISTERS KEEPER SERIES

Karleigh – A Story of Faith

Kaleigh – A Story of Patience

Kyna – A Story of Love

Karmyn – A Story of Hope (Coming 2021)

I hope you enjoyed reading about Kyna and Morgan. Who doesn't want a billionaire to fall in love with overnight. Stay connected with us for new releases, exclusive offers, free online reads and so much more.

Subscribe to my newsletter
www.authorlisawashington.com

Don't forget to follow and like us on
Facebook - @authorlisawashington
IG - @authorlisawashington
Pinterest - authorlisawashington